SADDLE TRAMPS

Corey Keogh believes that when you work with a man, ride with him, eat the same food and even love the same woman, you stay loyal to him. But then his gun-happy partner, Andy Givens, turns killer and sets about robbing banks. Then he forces his attentions on Corey's one love, Marly Pierce, and the day of reckoning has arrived ... Now friend must turn against friend, and it seems that only guns can sever the bond between them.

Books by Owen G. Irons
in the Linford Western Library:

THE DEVIL'S CANYON
THE DRIFTER'S REVENGE
GUNSMOKE MOUNTAIN
ON THE WAPITI RANGE
ROLLING THUNDER
THE BOUNTY KILLERS
SIX DAYS TO SUNDOWN

OWEN G. IRONS

SADDLE TRAMPS

Complete and Unabridged

LINFORD
Leicester

First published in Great Britain in 2008 by
Robert Hale Limited
London

First Linford Edition
published 2009
by arrangement with
Robert Hale Limited
London

British Library CIP Data

Irons, Owen G.
    Saddle tramps--(Linford western library)
    1. Western stories.
    2. Large type books.
    I. Title II. Series
    813.5'4–dc22

    ISBN 978–1–84782–812–5

1

It was a woman who started it all. I don't know if she meant to or not. Sometimes these things just happen when one of them is involved.

We had just dragged into Tulip, a little town not half as pretty as its name, me and Andy Givens. We had been working for six weeks on a round-up for that motherless Barry Slattery, had had just about enough of him and the Pocono Ranch life, taken our short-wages and after a word or two with Slattery and his honcho, Titus Evers, we had ridden at Andy's suggestion into the far distances to look for a place to spread our silver around a little before we had to figure out a way to earn some more.

It was a pattern Andy and I had fallen into, not much of a system for living long and well, but it suited us at that time. A week or two here, a few months there, depending on how long it took us to get tired of camp grub or fed up with the work, and we'd just look at each other, and without a word spoken we'd throw our saddles over our ponies' backs, collect our pay or whatever portion of it the tight-fisted boss felt like he could spare, and ride off toward the next hope of greener pastures, scattering silver dollars in our wake.

Put plainly, we were saddle tramps, me and Andy Givens. We weren't alone; there were thousands of men drifting the Western lands looking for the opportunity everyone said was waiting out here for us. If you could just find it.

We were still looking when Andy shot and killed a farmer named Miles Sturdevant at the Grange dance in Tulip. Me, I knew it meant trouble when we entered the meeting hall among all of those sodbusters and saw Andy's eyes nearly pop out of his head at the sight of Eva Pierce. There was no pulling Andy out of there. It would have been like trying to drag a bulldog away by his tail once he had his mind set on proceeding in the other direction.

'I have not ever, in my life seen a woman so perfectly put together,' Andy said. He stood, young and curly-haired, his boots positioned wide apart, his hat pushed back off his forehead and grinned all the way across the crowded room at Eva.

She smiled back and then turned her eyes away demurely. That smile was enough to give Andy all the encouragement that he needed. Andy, unlike me, was a handsome devil with flashing blue eyes and a mop of curly black hair. He thought of himself as a ladies' man and there were plenty of women who would second his opinion.

'Better back out of here, Andy,' I told him. 'Some of these farm boys are giving us the evil look.'

'Not until I've danced with that girl, Keogh.'

'I'm telling you it means trouble,' I warned him, but I never had any luck at reining Andy Givens in when he had his mind set, and I didn't on this occasion. He put a hand briefly on my shoulder then swaggered away through the overall-clad sodbusters in their farm shoes, his high-heeled cowboy's boots clicking arrogantly across the plank floor of the Grange house. I eased back toward the punchbowl which, fortunately, was near the door, and watched his progress.

'Friend of yours?' a voice at my shoulder asked quietly. I had just dipped out a cup of fruit punch and was raising the drink to my lips. I glanced at the owner of the voice, a man with slicked-down hair and small dark eyes. Years of following a plow had lent him a pair of shoulders about twice as thick as my own.

'I know him,' I had to admit, since Andy and I had come in together.

'Better tell him to fade, stranger. That's Eva Pierce, Bull Mosely's woman.'

I looked across the room to where

Andy, standing within friendly distance of the girl, his hat still tipped back, was grinning and chatting up Eva. It was a familiar game with Andy. The ladies were fond of his boyish charm and manly form, and he knew it.

'He's just introducing himself around,' I said. The farmer put a huge, hairy hand around my wrist and forced my arm down until the punch cup I had been holding clattered free of my grip and settled with a ringing sound on the cloth-covered table.

'I said that's Bull Mosely's woman,' the man with the expressionless face repeated.

'I'll tell him to lay off,' I promised, just to get the bearlike sodbuster to release my wrist.

I wasn't afraid of the farmer, understand, although I wouldn't have wanted to go rough-and-tumble with him. In my own world, on the range, I would have drawn my Colt, backed him off, and maybe if he didn't want to back off, simply cracked him above the ear with the barrel of my pistol. When he came to, we would more than likely just shake hands and forget it.

I didn't think they played by the same rules here, and as a stranger who had never so much as set foot in Tulip until an hour ago, I somehow didn't think they'd take such activity as socially acceptable.

Besides they had us outnumbered about fifty to one. I was willing to put a damper on my own impulses. The trouble was, Andy never was. He wasn't constitutionally able to pry himself away from a woman he'd set his sights on.

'I'll tell him,' I promised the big man.

'You do that,' the plowboy said. 'So I don't have to.' I nodded, tried a smile and brushed past him. As I did I felt that unnerving tingle of fear that sometimes crawls over a man in a bad position. It was something like being stripped naked in front of all these sodbusters.

He had lifted my Colt in passing and

now held it tightly clenched in his bear's paw. He smiled at me. Or, I think it was a smile. His vacant black eyes remained fixed on me. A second man approached us and I heard him ask, 'What's the trouble here, Bull?'

'No trouble, Miles. This pony-ornament is going to take care of things.'

I didn't like that remark either. From time to time farmers could get a little testy where cowhands were concerned. Especially when it was necessary to cut their fence wire to drive a herd through, trampling their crops in passing. Some people are just plain unreasonable. I didn't get any other smiles or words of welcome as I crossed the length of the social gathering toward Andy. He, on the other hand, was happily talking to Eva who was matching him smile for smile. Another girl who looked enough like Eva to be her younger sister had joined the group. Her eyes shone and she was scented with lilac. She, too, was smiling brightly as Andy unloaded his charm for their amusement.

I didn't have to look behind me to know that Bull Mosely's dark face was not wreathed in smiles.

'Let's be going, Andy,' I said, tapping him on the shoulder.

He glanced at me, shook his head dismissively and returned his attention to Eva. He said, 'The first thing you know, the bronc and I were both . . . have you met my friend Corey Keogh here? First thing you know — ' Andy continued.

'Andy,' I persisted. 'I just met the welcoming committee. We are not wanted here.'

'Tell 'em to go to hell,' Andy said, with that cheerful, cocky attitude which he dazzled women with.

'I tried.' I turned Andy half-around by his shoulder and told him seriously, 'I mean it, Andy. There's going to be trouble if we don't blow.'

'Keogh, old partner, when isn't there trouble when we land somewhere?'

I was about ready to give up on the

8

pleading and yank him out of there by his belt whether he liked it or not, but they didn't give me time. I heard the heavy approaching boots, clomping almost in unison across the long room. Bull Mosely was in the lead. Eva glanced that way, not surprised, not startled. She touched Andy's arm just then — lightly — but she might as well have lit a fuse to a stick of dynamite. Bull Mosely let loose a terrific bellow and charged forward, shouldering men and women aside as he came on. He still had my pistol in his hand. I saw him glance down at it as if he was just now remembering what it was for.

'Shake it, Andy. The locals are on the prod!'

Andy bit at his lower lip, studied the approaching mob and said to Eva, 'Thin-skinned bunch around here, aren't they?'

The girl put her hands on her slender hips and stamped her tiny foot as Bull approached, his eyes as dark as the interior of a coal mine at midnight.

'Now what!' she demanded of the hulking fanner.

'Now this — I told these two to get.'

'What gives you that right?' Eva asked, leaning toward the big man. 'Because I was enjoying a conversation with someone? I happen to enjoy meeting new people, *interesting* people,' she said.

That last remark was too much for Bull. I heard my gun clatter to the floor as he dropped it, slapped his left hand across Andy's holster and wrapped his right around Andy's throat, lifting him off the ground. Eva screamed, but I thought she was just a little delighted by the sudden action. Me, I was scared, plain and simple. We didn't know this man or his friends. For all we knew they made a habit of stringing up passing strangers just to watch them sky dance. I did know one thing — there was no way this was going to be a fair fight. I made the only reasonable move I could think of. I dove for my Colt.

A big foot was thrust out, tripping me. Skidding on elbows and knees, I nevertheless managed to reach out and grab my pistol. I had the hammer eared back and ready to drop on a primer by the time one of them bent over me with both fists clenched.

'I wouldn't do that, friend,' I warned him as he drew back his arm. 'You want to go home from this party alive, don't you?'

I didn't see the second man begin his move, and I couldn't guess where the hickory club in his hand had come from, but I saw it end its arc. The heavy length of lumber cracked my wrist and the pistol dropped free. Stars of pain sparkled behind my eyes, flashing in brilliant, many-colored spirals. I somehow had the presence of mind to grab the Colt with my left hand, and I was still holding it cocked and level when I lifted myself unsteadily to my feet, looking around, trying to find some way to back away from the dance-hall mob.

Something had changed. While I had briefly been distracted by having my wrist smashed to powder, Andy had

had enough, it seemed. Hoisted high in Bull Mosely's grip, strangling, struggling to free himself, Andy had come to his senses enough to realize the persuasive power of a knee driven with conviction into a man's groin.

I heard Bull howl, saw him back away, doubled up, saw Andy's hand flash down toward his holstered revolver and set himself, his breath coming in angry, strangled gasps. 'The first one to move catches lead,' Andy said, and if they didn't believe him, I did.

'Ready to mosey, Keogh?' Andy asked, scooping up his hat from the floor.

I could only nod. My mouth was dry, my head swam; my wrist was alive with fiery pain. By then Andy had spotted the rear door to the hall and we started that way, back to back. The glowering eyes of Bull Mosely followed us. Andy couldn't resist one last taunt.

'I'll be back for that dance, Miss Eva,' he said with a grin. 'Count on it.'

Andy heeled the door open while his

eyes remained fixed on the angry mob of farmers. He slipped out into the yard behind the building where the sodbusters had parked their wagons, and I followed. The bite of the chill evening air was sharp enough to clear my swimming head. It wasn't cold enough to cool the fiery pain in my wrist.

'Let's get going,' I begged Andy. 'I need to find a doctor.'

'Just a minute,' Andy said, indifferent to my suffering. 'They're working up their courage, waiting to see who'll be the first one through the door.'

No sooner had the words escaped Andy's lips than the first of the farmers shouldered the door open and burst through, Bull Mosely at their head. Andy was still grinning when he sprayed the doorframe with three rapid shots from his revolver, the .44s splintering the doorframe and ricocheting off into the distance. The oaken door was slammed shut and Andy punctured it with his remaining bullets.

'Now, Andy! Let's get out of here.'

But Andy was calmly taking fresh cartridges from his belt loops and reloading the smoking Colt he held. He watched the door for a long minute longer before deciding the fun was over.

'All right,' Andy said, 'let's find our ponies and shake the dust of this town off.'

Andy turned and strolled off as if he had no place urgent to go. Holding my injured wrist, I followed him in a half-blind stagger. The pain had returned and I felt like I would black out with each step. Andy had to stop and wait for me. Eventually he let me sling my good arm across his shoulders and he helped me along toward the stable where we had left out ponies. I got no sympathy for my condition, only one of Andy's laughing comments as we stumbled along the narrow alley.

'I feel sorry for the next cowboy who tries to go to a Grange dance in Tulip!'

That was Andy Givens for you. He could be a lot of fun to ride with. Then there were these other times . . .

★　★　★

We unsaddled our ponies on the low dark knoll at the hour of sunset. The wind had died down as the sun fell, but it was still cold. Even this far south, winter is no time for camping out. I found myself missing the smoky, male-smelling bunkhouse back at the Pocono Ranch. And, I considered, tight with his change though the Pocono owner, Barry Slattery, was, he would have taken one of his injured cowhands to see the doctor. Even if he took the cost of the visit out of your next pay packet.

I said that we unsaddled our ponies. More accurately, Andy unsaddled both horses as he had saddled them alone in Tulip while I stood watch in the doorway of the stable, gun in hand, waiting for any pursuit by the angry swarm of farmers. Apparently they had had enough of us, however, for we rode unmolested from the small town and far out on to the surrounding prairie.

'How's your wrist?' Andy asked with a small show of concern as we hunkered down near the tiny fire he had built.

'I'd cut my own arm off if it would get rid of the hurt,' I said as I sat cradling my double-sized wrist in my lap. 'I've got to get some help, Andy. I mean it.'

As if he had not heard me, Andy, a shadowy crouching figure before the flickering flames of the night-fire, said, 'Better shift your holster to your left side, Keogh. It'll give you a chance anyway . . . in the next dust-up we happen to fall into.'

I nodded, lay back and clumsily rolled up in my blanket to await the long night during which I knew I would not sleep. Lying sprawled on the hard ground, half-covered by my blankets, one of my feet furiously itching inside my battered boot, my empty stomach growling and my hand shot through with jagged pain, I began to reassess my choice of lifestyle. To a lesser extent, I was forced to reevaluate my choice of saddle partners. Andy Givens was hunkered down next to the fire, warming his hands by its feeble heat, whistling softly through his teeth.

I had almost made it — very nearly managed to fall asleep in the cold, pain-ridden night — when I heard Andy stir, pause listening, and leap to his feet, slicking his Colt from its holster.

'Somebody's coming in, Keogh,' he hissed.

I rolled over, pawing awkwardly for my gun with my left hand and got to my feet. I could hear it now too. The steady, heavy clopping of a horse's hoofs. I glanced at Andy and held up one finger questioningly. He frowned and shrugged. It seemed to be only one man. We crouched silently waiting his arrival.

'Hallo the camp!' the stranger called out, not too loudly and Andy answered him.

'Keep riding!'

17

'My horse is pretty beat down,' the lone rider said, still moving toward our camp. I could pick out the silhouette of man and horse against the low, flickering stars. 'Smelled your smoke. I was hoping you'd have coffee and grub.'

'Nothing to spare,' Andy said with irritability. The next sound was the ratcheting of his pistol's hammer, seeming unnaturally loud in the night. The stranger heard it as well.

'I'm harmless, friend!' he called out with a hint of laughter.

'Let him come in, Andy,' I said.

'Wait a minute . . . how many are you?' Andy inquired of the dark figure.

'Two, if you count my horse. What's the matter, friend? Somebody trailing you?'

'None of your damn business.'

'You're right,' the stranger answered, half-laughing again. 'I'm beat. I'm swinging down — Mind that trigger finger. If anyone is looking for you, a shot will sure bring them in a hurry.'

He was right, of course. I had

considered that. Andy hadn't. Andy Givens was apt to do things that way, act and then figure out what the results had been. Without holstering his pistol, he muttered, 'Come on in then. If you've got a rifle, leave it with your pony.'

The stranger — he was a tall man, and very thin — sauntered easily into the camp. He was carrying a small sack. With a glance at Andy and a nod to me, he squatted down near the dead fire and began prodding it to life.

'I said we had no coffee,' Andy said querulously.

'Brought my own,' the stranger said, holding up the small sack. 'Got any water in those canteens?'

I tossed him my canteen, seeing that Andy was still brooding, trying to make up his mind what ought to be done with the strange rider. After some prodding, the tiny fire caught fuel and sparked to life again.

'I'll be on my way after I have a cup and my horse has had the chance to blow. You don't really need to hold me under the gun, friend.' He poked at the small fire and eased the coffee pot toward the flames. 'Where are you boys heading?' he asked. Neither of us spoke. The truth was we didn't know. I wanted some information, however.

'There any towns up ahead?' I asked. My wrist was getting no better, would not get better without a doctor.

'Couple,' the stranger answered, keeping his eyes on the fire. 'Hemandez — that's a Mex town. OK if you palaver. It's about ten miles on, if you hold due west. After that ... ' He scratched his chin. 'There's a place called Tolliver.'

'Do they have a doctor?'

'I couldn't say, friend.' The little one-quart pot was already boiling. The visitor had put in only enough water for one cup of coffee. 'Hear about the trouble back in Tulip?' he asked, looking up abruptly. I saw Andy's face tighten. My stomach drew in on itself.

'No.' Andy was definite. 'We skirted that hick town.'

'You should've stopped,' the stranger said, and I saw that he had been eyeing my damaged wrist. 'They have a doctor *there*.'

'You talk a lot,' Andy commented.

'What trouble are you talking about?' I asked. The stranger filled his tin cup with coffee, sipped at it and replied.

'Man gunned down earlier back there. Got shot through a closed door. Bullet took him in the forehead. Damn shame,' he said, shaking his head.

'Did he have a name?' I asked. I could feel myself trembling. Andy's eyes were wider than normal.

'They called him Miles Sturdevant. Shot right through the door!'

'You already said that,' Andy growled.

'Sounds like it was an accident then,' I commented. The stranger looked at me over his coffee cup and smiled.

'Does it? Back in Tulip they're saying it was murder. Plain murder. Maybe whoever was shooting didn't intend to do it, but it's murder all the same. They'll surely hang those boys if they catch up with them.' The man tossed the few drops left in his cup on to the flames and watched the dregs sizzle and steam. Rising, he nodded his head and said, 'Thanks for the hospitality, men. I hope you find a doctor, son.' Then he touched the brim of his hat and we watched as he walked away into the night, his shadow merging with the long darkness of the night plains.

Andy started to follow him. I grabbed his arm as he passed me and hissed:

'No, Andy!'

'He knows who we are.'

'Sure he does, but he gave us warning, too. We've got to saddle up and ride.'

'I don't want to leave him behind to say what he knows,' Andy said, and by the feeble starlight I saw a wolfish glint in Andy's eyes. It was something new, a side of the wild cowhand I'd never seen before.

'Andy,' I said, tightening my restraining grip. 'What happened back then — in Tulip — we both know that it was an accident. If you do what you're think-ing it *will* be murder, plain murder.'

I don't know if I had convinced Andy or not. The matter became moot as we watched the stranger turn his horse and ride away, disappearing into the cold night. 'Let's ride, Andy,' I told him. 'We have to put some miles under our ponies before we have other guests.'

'All right. We'd better,' he agreed. 'Wouldn't the boys back at the Pocono have a good laugh if we got ridden down and strung up by a bunch of farmers forking mules and plow horses!' Andy laughed. He was his old cheerful self again. I smiled and started kicking my bed together.

It was funny, I thought, that Andy had been thinking of the Pocono Ranch and the boys back there, because that's exactly what I was thinking of again. Wishing that I was back there sleeping on my old swayed bunk, smelling man-sweat and tobacco.

Instead of being a murderer on the run.

2

Tolliver, if that was the town we were looking at as we sat our tired ponies on a grassy rise overlooking the cluster of buildings below us, wasn't anything its inhabitants were likely to brag about. A deeply-rutted main street with perhaps a dozen buildings on each side facing it like a nameless crowd, another twenty or thirty structures scattered at irregular intervals along a few rough side streets. There seemed to be no plan to the town, no common design to the buildings which were of adobe or brick or weather-grayed planks, some of them augmented by corrugated steel panels.

'Threw it up with whatever they had at hand, didn't they?' Andy asked sourly.

'Looks like.' I saw no flourishing farms, only half a dozen cattle gathered near one of the larger white houses. No sign of industry. It was hard to determine why Tolliver had been built where it was at all. But there was a river that snaked its way across the long valley. Its silver glint was bright in the morning sun. Maybe the early settlers had topped out the rise where we now sat, weary from months on the overland trail, spied the river and said, 'The hell with this pioneering. This is good enough for me,' and just stayed on.

I thought that the odds of the burg having a real doctor were slim, but I had to find out. I was feverish after our night ride. My hand was swollen so that my fingers looked like bloated crimson sausages and pain pulsed through all of my arm.

'What the hell,' Andy muttered. 'They must have beer at least.'

I wasn't giving any thought to beer or any other refreshment. Even the deep hunger gnawing at my stomach had ceased, overridden by the demanding pain. I got little sympathy from Andy, but I understood it. No one pays any attention to another man's toothache. Somehow, people aren't built that way. To me, however, there was nothing else in the world that meant a thing beyond relieving the pain that I was carrying. I thought that if all else failed, there might be a barber with Chinese opium on his shelf alongside his leeches. It wasn't unheard of. In many towns the barber was the only man of medicine to be found. And opium had comforted many a dying man on his trail to the grave.

However, I had never seen a barber set a broken wrist.

'Let's get on down there, Andy,' I said.

The horses' hoofs whispered through the long grass. The new sun was warm on my chilled back as it rose higher behind us. Dark shadows stretched out from the squat collection of buildings. In the far distance the line of snow-capped mountains reflected the morning light with the brilliance of mirrors.

I heard a dog yapping somewhere as we neared the foot of the main street, saw two kids with fishing poles walking toward the river. A storekeeper was sweeping the section of plankwalk in front of his store. He glanced up in surprise as we trailed our ponies into town. Strangers, I considered, must be something of a rarity in Tolliver. I didn't like that. We would be too easily remembered if anyone should come looking for us here.

'You have a doctor in this town?' Andy called out to the storekeeper and after a moment's thought, the man lifted a stubby finger up the street. 'Looks like you're in luck,' Andy said. He grinned. 'And so am I!'

He nodded toward the badly plastered adobe-block building across the street. Two horses stood patiently at its hitchrail and the door stood open. Above the doorway the word 'saloon' was inexpertly painted.

'Andy — ' I cautioned.

'I know! Be careful! Don't start any

trouble! Keogh, you always expect the worst of me.'

He laughed and turned his pony's head toward the saloon. I watched him go. He was right — I did always expect the worst where Andy was concerned. He didn't set out deliberately to find trouble, but he had a way of drawing it to him like a magnet. I rode on, scanning each building, looking for the doctor's office.

When I found it, the front door was standing open — apparently the folks in Tolliver liked their fresh air. I called out, got no reply and, removing my hat, crossed the sagging plank floor of the gray room. There was a desk, a swivel chair with a leather back, a medical chart posted on the wall and a filing cabinet with a veneered-wood face.

'What!'

The little man at the interior doorway appeared startled to find me there. He was bent with age, white-haired and moved with a shuffling gait. In his hand he held a plate of ham and eggs which he carried to his desk and placed carefully down. He began eating without saying a word more to me.

'Sir,' I asked, 'are you the doctor?'

Without looking up from his plate he nodded. Glancing around I spied a spindly wooden chair and seated myself waiting for the old man to finish his breakfast.

'What is it?' he asked, sawing away at his thick slice of ham with a dull knife.

'Broke my wrist,' I said, holding it up.

'I'll look at it in a minute,' the doctor answered. 'A man has to eat. Now that sounds like nothing, but a lot of people don't seem to be able to accept that simple fact.' He went on some more about feeding the human form, but I wasn't really listening. My broken wrist still commanded all of my attention. Finally, his utensils clattered down against his plate, and dabbing at his mouth with a napkin, the doctor pulled a pair of spectacles from his vest pocket, rose shakily, and came to where I sat waiting. He picked up my swollen red hand, turned it over and prodded it gently. I winced with the pain his fingers caused.

'Shattered. You should have had it set yesterday,' he said in a scolding voice.

'There wasn't a doctor around,' I told him.

'All right — ' He clicked his tongue. 'We'll see what we can do for you. I'm going to have to manipulate the bones, son. I'm afraid it will hurt.'

'It already hurts,' I said weakly.

'This is going to hurt a lot more,' he promised. 'I'm going to give you some laudanum and when that starts to work its evil magic, I'll proceed.' He went to a glass-fronted case filled with apothecary jars and colored glass bottles, removed one of these and studied its label closely.

'What do you do for a living, son?' he asked.

'I'm a cowhand.'

'Not any more,' he said dourly. I took it for a joke.

'Not until this is healed, you mean?' I

said with an imitation smile.

'Not ever,' the doctor said. 'Unless you can form a loop, rope a calf and tie it up with one hand.'

'When my right hand is healed — '

'Son,' the doctor said bluntly, 'that hand is never going to be useful again.'

★ ★ ★

With my heavily splinted hand bound up with about six yards of gauze, a bottle of laudanum in my hip pocket and a dizzy, sick feeling on me, I went out of the doctor's office to face the brilliant morning sunlight. I led my horse up the street where now a few men on horseback and a wagon taking on goods at the store populated the wretchedly rutted thoroughfare. There were two wooden chairs placed on the boardwalk in front of the saloon and in one of these sat Andy, tilted back with a mug of beer in his hand. I was pleased to see him by himself. Even Andy Givens has trouble getting into a scrape when he's alone.

'What'd the doctor say?' Andy asked, as I eased myself into the other chair.

'He told me that my cattle-working days are done,' I said grimly. 'Says that the plowboy smashed my wrist up good and proper.'

'Tough,' Andy said, and he took a sip of his beer. His boyish eyes flashed at me. 'What do you figure on doing then, Keogh?'

'I don't know,' I answered dismally. 'I'll think about it when my mind is clearer. He's got me doped up pretty good right now.' I showed him the laudanum bottle and he nodded.

'We'd better keep riding, Keogh. I wish we could stable up the ponies, but I don't like this situation much. The horses are pretty beat down; I figure that what we can do is ride somewhere along the river, water them and let them graze.'

'It's all we can do,' I agreed.

'I'll get us a gunny sack full of supplies at that little store we passed.

We should avoid towns for a little while. That's where they'll look for us.'

'You think they'll keep coming?' I asked worriedly. Inadvertently, I looked toward the head of town as if a posse of farmers might appear there at any moment. Andy nodded, placed his mug beside his boot on the plankwalk and answered:

'They'll keep coming. Maybe they'll hire someone to come after us, but they won't leave it alone, I don't think.'

I didn't either, no matter what I hoped. Two days ago I had just been a laboring, disgruntled cowboy with two silver dollars in his jeans. Now I was a maimed killer on the run and my pockets were stripped bare. I had to tell Andy.

'I gave the last of my ready cash to the doctor, Andy. I can't chip in for the supplies.'

'I figured as much,' Andy said, stretching his arms high in the air as he yawned deeply. 'Don't give it a thought, Keogh. I'm the banker in this outfit.'

My eyes narrowed questioningly. Andy grinned and reached inside his blood-red shirt. Around his neck was the little leather sack he always wore there to carry his spending cash. Now he tugged the neck of the sack open and let a few coins spill out into the palm of his rough hand.

The gold gleamed brightly in the slanting morning sunlight. Stunned, I could not say a word for a minute. Then, after Andy had tucked the sack inside his shirt again, I managed to stutter:

'That's Barry Slattery's money, isn't it!'

'Not *now*, obviously,' Andy said, getting to his feet. 'Why'd you think I was in such a hurry to ride out of Pocono, Keogh?'

'I didn't think that you'd robbed Slattery!'

'That's the last time he'll short *me* on my pay,' Andy said firmly. 'The man was a crook, and you know it, Keogh.'

I had to scurry to follow him down

on to the street where he had unlooped his horse's reins and started walking toward the store.

'The other boys — ' I said breathlessly. 'That money was for their pay, too, Andy. Charley and all the boys out at the line camps.'

'Slattery can make it up,' Andy said carelessly. 'He's got thousands stuffed away in the bank.'

'He'll be mad as hell, Andy! So will the boys. All of the Pocono Ranch crowd will be looking for us!'

'They'll never catch us,' Andy said confidently. 'No one is going to catch up with us. Quit worrying, Keogh.'

I followed his shadow wordlessly to the store, waiting with the horses as Andy tramped inside to make his purchases. My head was still whirling from the laudanum. Spinning and spinning. I couldn't sort through it all. Why hadn't Andy told me what he'd done? Now we not only had the town of Tulip after us but all of Pocono Ranch. Slattery would not take being robbed lying down. Nor would his foreman, the bad-tempered Titus Evers. For that matter the boys — our friends — would be sore as hell when their pay packets were empty, even if they did get their coin a few days, a week, later. I leaned my head against the heated flank of my horse and stifled a moan.

I lifted my head as the sound of Andy's boot heels clicking across the plankwalk sounded. Whistling, a sack of provisions over his shoulder, he looked quite pleased with himself. He was, of course. Andy, I had long known, was a rogue of a man, cocky and carefree, unaware of anyone else's idea of what was proper and civilized. That was what made him fun to be around; he was engaging company, always quick with a laugh and handy with the girls.

It's just that this was the first time I had realized how utterly amoral he was, a man without faults in his own mind because he had long ago convinced himself that he was free of arbitrary bonds and entitled to whatever gifts life brought his way.

Andy tied the provision sack on to his saddle horn and swung aboard his leggy appaloosa pony. I lifted myself clumsily into leather and followed him down the street.

'Here,' Andy told me as we again reached the saloon, and he started his horse up a narrow alley beside it. Shrugging, I followed.

There was a woman in a striped Mexican skirt and white blouse worn off the shoulder behind the building, the reins to a buckskin horse in her hand. She smiled at Andy with lips that were a little too full. Dark eyes sparkled in her round face as she looked up at him. A quiver of foreboding swam through my dulled mind. I looked to Andy pleadingly. But I already knew . . .

'Carmen is going with us,' Andy said easily. 'She's tired of working in the *cantina*.'

I had left Andy to his own devices for only half an hour, no more. Quite enough time for him to strike an alliance, charm a bored local girl stuck in a dull job in a drab town with no prospect of ever leaving.

I didn't raise my voice to protest. What would have been the point to it? The woman — Carmen — swung on to her buckskin horse, flashing a lot of leg as she did, and Andy guided us past the backs of the buildings and out of the small town, leading us toward an uncertain and unpromising future beyond.

We camped that morning along the river which Carmen had told us was named Mariposa Creek and which eventually merged with the Arkansas River. Having eaten, I sat watching the horses munch grass. The sun was warm and soothing through the cottonwood trees and the narrow river made lulling sounds as it passed. With my mind numbed by the concoction of alcohol and opium the doctor had given me in Tolliver, the struggles, the long night ride, I wasn't able to keep my eyes open any longer.

Glancing at Andy and Carmen who

were happily sharing a blanket near the bank of the river, I dragged my bedroll up into the shifting shadows beneath the trees where a light breeze blew, toying with the upper reaches of the cottonwoods.

I slept for hours, but eventually the returning pain in my arm brought me awake and I had to sit up and reach for the little blue bottle of laudanum. Sipping it, I saw that Andy and Carmen were up and active, saddling the horses, so I dragged myself to my feet and started that way, glancing at the slowly descending sun, the distant Rocky Mountains.

'Carmen says we can make Colorado in a couple of days,' Andy said as I met him. He gave the cinch of my saddle an extra tug and stepped away from my roan, patting its neck. 'You got me doing all the work, Keogh!' Andy laughed. 'Boy, I don't know how you're going to get along without me!'

Carmen, leading her hammer-headed buckskin, walked toward us, her round head bowed, her skirt rustling in the wind. I said nothing as Andy started toward her. They bent their heads together in private conversation and I heard Andy laugh again — that reckless, wild laugh of his. Carmen, it seemed, was trying to encourage Andy to move faster, to hit the Colorado trail sooner rather than later. Andy was in no hurry. He seldom was.

I heard a brief spate of Spanish from Carmen, saw her gesturing back toward the town. I don't speak much of the language, but I was sure I heard the word *esposa*, which isn't far removed from its English equivalent. I waited as Andy separated himself from the woman then sidled up to join me.

Andy was busy saddling his appaloosa pony and just slid me a glance.

I said, 'I heard a few words of that, Andy. Don't tell me that she's married!'

'I guess so,' Andy said, 'but she doesn't like him much.'

Which justified her running away with Andy in his mind. To Andy the road to happiness was just following your impulses. I shook my head violently.

'He might come after her, Andy!' Which was just what we needed. It seemed we already had half the territory looking for our scalps.

'You're worried, aren't you?' Andy said, frowning. He stood with his arms folded, his back leaning against the flank of his tall appy. He shrugged. 'You're probably right, Keogh. Tell her to beat it.'

Andy returned his attention to his pony. He had made a decision; that was that. He now expected me to tell the woman he had just seduced away from her husband to go home and forget it had ever happened.

Callous when stated that way, it meant nothing at all to Andy. Carmen had come along voluntarily. She was old enough to know better. He had just changed his mind, that was all. A man has the right to change his mind.

'I can't do it, Andy,' I said, looking

41

toward the river where the brown-eyed, hopeful woman stood watching Andy, her savior, her way out of the dull, soul-strangling life she was leading in Tolliver. Andy didn't argue with me. We seldom argued. He just gave me a look as if I was completely useless and started toward the girl while I waited with our horses.

I heard nothing of the exchange. As I watched, however, Carmen's eyes grew wide and panic overtook her. What was she to tell her husband? Her fingers clutched at Andy, but he shook her off. I could see the distaste on his face. Frowning, he stepped to the head of the buckskin horse, slipped the bit and unbuckled the throat latch. With Carmen clawing at him, pleading, Andy flung bridle and reins into the river, adjusted his hat and walked back toward me, leaving the astonished woman behind.

'Now let's see her follow us,' Andy said, and he swung easily into the saddle and started his appaloosa away, across the river. I hesitated, but what could I do or say? I swung clumsily aboard my roan pony and followed Andy Givens across the Mariposa and up the Colorado trail.

I don't know why it came over me just then, as I walked my pony through the river shallows, his hoofs sending up silver fans of water, the long shadows across the land beginning to gather and the sunset light to dull and diffuse, but it did:

I was going to die if I continued to ride the range with Andy Givens.

3

I thought about my problem all the long evening as we crossed the high-grass prairie, aiming toward the lofty purple mountains to the west. By the time we made night camp, the conclusion I had reached was inescapable. Andy was a wild man, literally. He was not malicious, but his utter disregard for civilized codes was leading us along a path of destruction. His rash courage, such a virtue on the untrammeled lands when herding cattle, taming wild mustangs or fighting Indians, proved to be his greatest fault in other environs.

Among settled people he was, even without intention, only a rogue puma asking to be shot down. Or hung by his neck.

There hadn't been more than five minutes that day when I hadn't been looking across my shoulder, expecting pursuit. By the people from Tulip, by Barry Slattery's Pocono crew, by Carmen's wronged husband. Our enemies, it seemed, were legion and Andy — careless and untamed — could only lead us into more grief.

We had decided to risk a small fire. Again we had camped on a knoll to enable us to watch the backtrail. It had only been a few days, but it felt as though we were establishing a pattern for the rest of our lives. Men on the run, forced to avoid settlements, ready with our guns.

My head throbbed. My arm flared up with pain each time the soothing influence of the laudanum faltered. I did not wish to see what my hand and wrist looked like under the bundle of dirty bandaging. My Colt rode awkwardly on my left hip in my right-handed holster. I wouldn't even be able to put up a decent fight if the hunters came down upon us.

'Buck up, Keogh!' Andy said, pouring more coffee into my tin cup. 'You look like you've been trampled down and left to soak in buffalo muck.'

'That's pretty much the way I feel, Andy,' I said looking up at him through the flickering firelight.

'Your hand is bound to heal up. A few more days and you'll be your old self.'

'I doubt it,' I answered miserably. It had to be said, so I plunged ahead with my thoughts. 'Andy . . . we've got to split up. It's better for both of us.' Andy was frowning, meditatively turning his coffee cup in his hands. I went on. 'If you'll trust me with half the provisions, maybe let me have four or five dollars cash money, I'd be able to make my own way come morning.'

I waited. For anything: an understanding nod, a slow, careful curse, an angry explosion, but when Andy's answer did come it was just a roaring, pitying laugh. He leaned forward and patted my shoulder.

'It's that laudanum that the doctor gave you to take, Keogh. That's what's doing the talking. Corey Keogh, you've never been a nervous man before! You've got to stick with me, friend,' Andy said, lowering his voice. I sensed a sort of uncertainty or nervousness in his voice that I did not entirely understand. He told me:

'You can't make it out here by yourself, Keogh. Not with that hand, penniless and hungry. No — I'm not splitting up the provisions, and I need what coin I have. You're stuck with me, *compañero*. We ride together.' Quietly, he added something even more disturbing, 'I need a witness.'

I rolled up in my blankets making my own plans. I was getting shot of Andy, I just hadn't figured out how to do it — not out here in a thousand square miles of empty land, crippled as I was. The laudanum produced swirling, disturbing images in my mind, thoughts that struggled but could not force themselves into the shape of a proper dream and after awhile I fell into a merciful, pitch-black sleep.

The angry voice brought me awake. I don't know how many times the big man had shouted before his roaring incomprehensible words brought my drugged mind to alertness. I was aware of a broad-shouldered man in a tight-fitting Spanish suit standing over me. He had a wide-brimmed sombrero dangling down his back on a draw-string. He had a big-bored Colt .44 in his hand and his stubby thumb was drawing the hammer back as I sat up in bed, wildly searching for my own revolver which was not where it was habitually positioned.

The man fired. I threw myself to the earth and tried to roll to my feet. Then the second gun opened up. Three shots, four, flame blossoming in the night, the peals of gunfire echoing like thunder down a canyon. The big man crumpled and fell unmoving to the dark earth.

'He wasn't much of a shot, was he?' Andy Givens said, nudging the stranger with his boot toe. Neither of us knew, but we each had guessed who the interloper was. Andy commented dryly, 'I guess Carmen won't have to worry about him any more.'

In the morning, after we had built a rough cairn to cover the dead Mexican, we again saddled and started on our way, the rising sun coloring the eastern skies crimson and stark purple. I had nothing to say on this morning. I had refused coffee, refused the pan-bread Andy had fried while Carmen's spouse still lay visible, contorted next to our camp. It was Andy who broke our uneasy silence as side-by-side we continued our ragged odyssey across the western plains.

'That should be a lesson to you, Keogh. Last night I told you that you couldn't take care of yourself! Make up your mind that you're stuck with me, old friend.' His look was vaguely threatening. I didn't understand it. Even when his blue eyes danced with merriment at the sight of a herd of fifty or so pronghorn antelopes making their bouncing way across our trail, I still felt the coldness behind his smiles.

I was beginning to feel like a prisoner.

It takes nothing to gun a man down and leave his unidentified body out on the plains, leave it to the scavengers and the buzzards, finally to the ants and even smaller guests at the feast of the dead. It was an everyday occurrence out there, in those days. But it was sickening all the same.

I had now adopted a new attitude and was sickened by that as well. Considering all that had gone before, desperate to survive, I found myself catering to Andy Givens, agreeing with any wild notion that might enter his head.

And all the time looking for a way to escape his threatening company.

On the fifth day of our run I could stand it no more and began unwinding the filthy, cumbersome bandages from my hand under Andy's amused gaze. What I found underneath was a purplish swollen bundle of meat and bone looking something like a dead bloated crab. I didn't even try to flex my fingers, not then. I left the gauze, the splint and the little blue laudanum bottle behind me on the prairie.

'They're still back there,' Andy said that afternoon as we continued our trek toward the snow capped mountains which seemed to remain constantly distant, but to double in enormity with each passing day.

I nodded. 'I've seen them. They're not gaining any ground, though,' I said, looking back toward the group of dark riders, far behind us, indistinguishable so far as detail, but all the more menacing for that.

'They're waiting for us to stop somewhere.' Andy squinted at me from the shadow of his hatbrim. 'No more towns for us for awhile. Good thing we have plenty of provisions still. And no night camps! We ride as long as the ponies can find their way in the dark.'

'If the horses give out,' I told Andy. 'We're done.'

'Yeah,' he answered, 'aren't we?'

Whoever it was that was following us, their horses would be as weary as ours, I was thinking. But they, of course, would have the option of trading for fresh mounts in some hamlet along the route, if one could be found. We could not stop now.

To our surprise we now discovered that copper strands had been strung overhead along the road we were following. The telegraph had come to our primitive land almost overnight. The singing wire could already have sent word about us ahead.

'It's all that gold they've found in Colorado,' Andy conjectured. He lifted his chin toward the strands of wire. 'They said that they've dug up more gold and silver along the Comstock Lode than has been found in Africa and Europe for the last twelve centuries. These money traders in the East want to know what's happening in Denver and Leadville.'

I didn't answer. I didn't know if

Andy's opinions were based on anything other than bunkhouse gossip. It seemed he might be right. It wasn't, I discovered, the telegraph or the Eastern ore magnates that had captured Andy's imagination and prompted his remarks.

'They say that in Denver some of those mine bosses have built houses with indoor plumbing — and all of the fixtures are of solid gold, Keogh,' he went on.

'Seems a waste,' I said. I couldn't think of anything else to say.

'Makes you think, though, doesn't it?' Andy turned slightly in the saddle. 'On the plains a man might risk a stagecoach holdup, dying in a storm of gunfire if it goes wrong, for a measly five hundred bucks. One bank alone in Denver, they say, has a hundred million dollars in its vaults . . . that does make a man think.'

If my mind hadn't been made up before, it was now. I had to get shot of Andy Givens at any cost.

At noon-high the next day I saw

them. A body of sixteen wagons, I counted, just around forty head of cattle, six drovers and a couple of outriders rolling slowly westward. Andy was riding with his head down. We were both pretty beat up, the trail having been long and water spare. I didn't think he saw the distant collection of pioneers. He gave no indication of it.

It was in my mind, as I have said, to get shot of Andy and shake my shadow free of the trailing riders behind us, whoever they might prove to be. What better place to conceal myself than among the pilgrims on a wagon train? Once among the settlers I would look like anyone's brother or husband, not stick out like I was now alone out on the long prairie.

I kept glancing that way all into the afternoon, waiting for my chance to shed Andy and see if I could join up with the settlers who would likely welcome anyone with an extra gun to defend their wagons. At least they would have food and water. I had none of my own, Andy having put the shutters up on the pantry door. I waited to make my move, drifting carefully away from Andy as twilight began to settle across the plains. I might not have told you this directly, but Andy Givens was no man to underestimate. He had seen those wagons and seemed to have been reading my mind.

'Suppose we go ahead and catch up with the wagon train when they've got their night fires lit, Keogh? We can slip away from whoever it is following on our back-trail. Come up with some story we can tell those greeners.'

I only nodded, feeling my hope of escape flatten, fold and deflate.

Near to sundown, Andy and I, still joined at the hip, veered from our trail and heeled our ponies toward the wagon encampment.

'Gentlemen?' the stranger with the shotgun said as we reached the busy camp where the settlers were setting up for evening meals, rounding up the kids and hushing the babies. Cattle, gathered into a circle, lowed quietly. These were mostly white-face steers, and a few milk cows, unlike the wild longhorns Andy and I had long argued with, and which were impossible to bed if they were not in the mood.

People cows, not beef cattle. Herefords and a few Jerseys, not the wild-eyed Texas breeds. The settler with the scattergun who had stopped us seemed more like the longhorn steers we were accustomed to.

I let Andy do the talking. He was born to shine people up.

'Sorry if we've startled you, friend,' Andy was saying. 'My friend and I, Mr Corey Keogh here, were out mustanging with a few of our friends. Had us a fair-sized gather of wild ponies when we got jumped. Indians. Think it must have been some Cheyenne that strayed from the reservation. It was chaos, brother! Lost our wild horses and most of our friends back there. We've been dragging the line for close to three days now, and we sure would appreciate coffee and a place to bed for the night.'

The story was neither too unusual or too wild to be believed. Especially not the way Andy told it, with his sincere eyes and frank smile. Me, I would have stumbled over my tongue on the lie and made a mess of things. The man with the shotgun was sympathetic.

'I guess we can keep you. Stay away from the women and our horses, and you're welcome.'

'We aren't that kind, mister!' Andy said as if his character had been impugned. 'My friend and I were three years in the cavalry helping folks like you across the plains.'

He got away with that one, too. The man muttered an apology and let us pass. Andy gave me a broad wink. 'My theory is, if it helps, tell 'em you're the president's brother.'

We had settled into our blankets and were watching as the campfires burned low, safe within the ring of wagons, with no sign on the pursuing men on our trail. Our stomachs were full and the prairie night was almost balmy. That didn't mean that our troubles were at an end.

I had seen her too.

You could not forget a face like Eva Pierce's. I felt as if I had been hit between the eyes by a sledgehammer when Andy and I went strolling in the twilight and came across the two girls from Tulip. Sure enough, it was Eva Pierce and the girl I had taken for her sister back there at the Grange hall. The younger one smiled shyly, Eva quite brazenly, with the secret knowledge she held dancing in her eyes. Andy and I had merely touched our hats and walked on, but for a long while after he was deep in thought.

'Well, well,' he murmured once as we traveled on. 'What do you think of that?'

I thought it was the end of us. I reflected on our situation as I lay in my blankets, listening to the sounds of the settlers' families as they made their night preparations, scolding a kid,

making small complaints and sometimes a little love-whisper passing
between them.

Eva Pierce! And I had seen that look
again in Andy's eyes. I wondered
— could it be that the men we thought
were pursuing us were not following *us*
at all? Could it be that it was the girls
they were chasing after? If so, that only
meant that we were in a worse fix than
before. Because if some of those
farmers out of Tulip were chasing them
down, Bull Mosely was bound to be at
their head, and finding me and Andy
among the settlers would only convince
him that his crazy jealousy was justified.

Then, too, his friend Miles Sturdevant had been killed in the melee and
Mosely would feel obligated to avenge
his death. All in all we seemed to have
landed in a more precarious situation
than we had started from. Tossing and
turning in my bed as the night sounds
quieted, with only the barking of the
dogs when they responded to the
yapping of prowling coyotes, the crying

of one colicky baby, I became more determined than ever to break with Andy Givens. I had seen the way he had looked at Eva Pierce and noticed the answering signal in her eyes.

I was riding a trail to perdition with the devil himself as my guide.

After midnight I had determined what my course of action had to be. My only resources were my weary roan horse and whatever loads remained in my Henry repeating rifle and my Colt, slung ridiculously on my left hip, but I had lived off game and roots before — not well, but I had survived. I could do it again even crippled-up as I was.

Andy was sleeping soundly, as he always did, deep in a conscienceless dream when I rolled out shortly after midnight, the stars silver-bright, gleaming in a cobalt sky. I didn't bother to try rolling my blankets, but slipped away into the night with them folded over my arm. I wanted my roan and my saddle, nothing more. I crept from the wagon camp.

And walked almost directly into the woman.

'Please,' she whispered, 'take us, too.'

It was the girl I had supposed to be Eva Pierce's younger sister. Her eyes were starlit, her expression pleading. Her words were broken by emotion. I made no response. I had none to give. She was small, much tinier than I remembered. I could make out little of her features in the darkness. A small nose, generous mouth and expressive star-bright eyes. Her hand was on my elbow and I shook it off. The night was still, and we were alone where we should not have been. She was a young woman terribly frightened of something.

I tried to put a rough edge in my voice.

'I don't know what you're talking about, lady. You must have me mistaken for someone else.'

'No,' she said, looking up at me. 'No I don't!' She went on as I looked around nervously, wishing I were anywhere else in the world. Her hand tightened on my arm. 'Your name is

Corey Keogh. You've fallen in with a man who's constantly heading for trouble. But you stand by him because he is your friend. Now you've had enough — you feel like you have to sneak away rather than hurt his feelings. We have to sneak away too. My sister and me. You are brave and you are loyal, Corey Keogh. That is how I know I can trust you.'

Well, she had my head spinning. I don't know how else to say it. She was right about a part of what she was saying, guessing at another part of it, totally confused about what kind of man I was. I never could shine as a hero. I was nothing but a saddle tramp and I knew it.

'Please?' she asked, standing so near to me that I could smell the yellow lye soap on her and something else — a hint of the lilac scent I remembered from the Grange hall.

'I don't know what you mean,' I said. 'I'm leaving, lady, on my own. I've enough troubles.'

'He'll kill Eva!'

'Who? Andy? He wouldn't — '

'No,' she said desperately. 'Not him — I know what Andy is — I mean Bull Mosely! Bull will kill Eva. She's . . . shamed his manhood.' Her eyes turned down and shifted away. I wasn't sure that I knew what she meant, although I could have taken a guess.

'There's another man, Corey . . . with Eva, there's always another man. She's on her way to meet him. In Colorado.'

'There's no reason for you to go, is there?' I asked more sharply than I intended. Her eyes flashed.

'She's my *sister*!' she answered, and I knew that it was enough reason for her. The question in my mind was: why me? And what could she expect me to do? It was all quite ridiculous, and I told her so. I was a man alone with only a pony and a pocketful of .44s. I was no match for the long plains, the rough mountains ahead, the band of men behind us.

'You're safer here with the wagon train,' I said.

'No!' She was emphatic. 'Why would

they fight for us? People they barely know? Bull will have a tale concocted — a runaway bride, something like that, and the men will laugh and let him take her away. Now Andy Givens has arrived! Bull can name him as the man who has run off with his woman. And you know Andy much better than I, but will he not let himself be prodded into a gunfight?'

'Yes,' I said soberly, 'he would.'

'Then we have three lives at stake here,' the girl said to me from out of the star shadows. 'Eva's, Andy Givens's . . .

'And?' I said.

'And my own, Corey Keogh. If my sister, if Eva . . . if something happened to her, I wouldn't be able to carry on alone.'

And she began to weep. It was too much. I would have broken down and accepted her improbable proposition if I still hadn't retained a crumb of common sense. Why do their tears affect us so? And can they produce them on demand to make their

64

argument stronger? I backed away a step and said, 'I've got to be going, girl.' I shrugged out of her hands and stalked unhappily to the remuda where my weary roan pony had been staked out with the rest of the settlers' horses.

It took a while for me to find my saddle in the stack of leather the wrangler had built, but in fifteen minutes I was on my big horse's back, breathing free, ready for whatever the long night ahead might hold for me. But there they were, ready and waiting for me before I had touched spurs to the roan.

'Here we are,' the young girl said. Eva Pierce flashed one of her brilliant smiles at me, and with sour curses boiling up inside of me, I led our party of three out into the dark distances of the long Kansas plains.

4

An hoot-owl had dived low on broad wings and swooped at my head, mistaking it for some small prey. My pony was unresponsive to the reins. I had to argue with him to continue his sullen plodding. Eva Pierce who had spent an hour steadily talking about how romantic and exciting a showdown between Andy and Bull Mosely would be, now rode in a half-doze, swaying in her side-saddle, the fur-lined hood of her amber-colored coat obscuring most of her face. The young lady at my side continued her disconnected chatter. She had thanked me two dozen times for my heroism and I was tired of it. There was nothing heroic about being ambushed by two frustrated, frightened women and impressed into service. Maybe Andy could have handled this situation well. All I could feel was the weary striding of my roan and the grating of my nerves.

'I didn't expect you to be such a grumbly man, Corey Keogh,' I was told by the young lady.

'This is not exactly a pleasure, miss.'

'I see ... ' The woman was thoughtfully silent for a minute. 'Your heart has been broken.'

'What in — What do you mean?'

'Somewhere, sometime, a beautiful girl shattered your dreams and now you have become ... '

'Grumbly.'

'Exactly!' she said, pleased with herself for having solved my condition. 'Who was this girl? Do you want to talk about it?'

'No. Look — Mary Lou, isn't that what I heard your sister call you? I'd rather talk about how we're going to survive, outrun Bull Mosely and his friends, make our way to Colorado — '

'Marly,' she interrupted. 'Only my sister still calls me Mary Lou, though that's my given name. Everyone calls me Marly.'

'Do they? That's fine.' I was angry and not doing a good job of holding it in. 'Look, Marly, a man alone out here has a chance. Game, enough graze and occasional water for his pony. One man can survive with luck. Then we have those — ' I lifted my chin toward the looming bulk of the great Rocky Mountains, stark and clear in the night with their 14,000 foot thrust despite the distance. 'We have to consider how even to imagine we're going to trek that mountainous country where game is not so plentiful, where winter comes early and hard.'

'You *are* a pessimist!' Marly said.

'And a grump.'

'That, too,' Marly said. 'For now, though, Corey Keogh, we had better just keep riding, for they are behind us. The men with the guns are on our trail again.'

She was right. As we paused to let our horses breathe, I could see, even in that poor light, enough of the thin veil of dust rising off the plains to indicate a large body of men following in our tracks. I was no longer grumpy, just plain scared, for these men meant to ride us down and probably to kill me over an affair I had nothing to do with.

Not for the last time I solemnly cursed Andy Givens and his rogue ways.

As a rule of thumb, traveling through life, I have always figured that just when you think things can't get any worse, they will.

Now as we continued on our way toward the bulk of the Rockies we picked up some traveling companions I did not care for. Three prairie wolves, and these skulking strangers seemed to have their minds set on us as a possible prey. One snap of their jaws at a pony's hock could leave it crippled and down, and us without a horse. Denver was a long way to walk.

I had used my pocketknife to saw away the front flap of my holster now that I had switched it to my left side, but had no confidence in my ability to shoot accurately with my Colt in that fashion. A long gun was slow in positioning and aiming, and so the wolves continued to worry me as they slunk along behind us, waiting for some opportunity to disable one of the horses.

My rule of thumb continued to prove its reliability in the next ten minutes. I did not expect it when it happened although I had been concerned with the possibility. In a rush the three silver wolves charged at us, their eyes excited with feral eagerness. In their blood was the knowledge of how to take down a bison, an elk with quick, vicious snaps of their heavy jaws to the animal's tendons, and they surged upon us with that confidence.

I pawed at my holster, failed to make purchase and heard the shots from an unexpected quarter roar, the echoes rolling across the long prairie as one of the wolves went down. A second escaped on a crippled leg, the other skittered away in a loping run.

Rule of thumb . . . Andy Givens drew up beside us on his lathered appaloosa pony and grinned at me, smoke still leaking from the muzzle of his revolver.

'I told you that you just can't get along without me, Keogh,' Andy said. Then, holstering his weapon, he turned his eyes on Eva Pierce. 'Hello, Honey. What made you take off like that?'

'I don't want any more trouble,' Eva managed to say. Her eyes were fixed on the dead wolf, not on Andy. 'Bull Mosely is trouble. But you . . . you're *all* trouble, Andy.'

Andy, being himself, only laughed. 'That's me, I guess! That doesn't mean I'm not a good man to have around in a pinch. Ask my friend Keogh here.'

All of which just seemed like banter, mild boasting. But, you would have had to be there. Even by the thin glow of starlight I could see Andy's eyes as they shifted, refocused and came to rest on Marly. If Eva didn't want him, the look said, maybe her little sister would take an interest in him.

I wasn't the only one to notice the look in Andy's eyes. Marly deliberately eased her pony closer to mine and asked, 'Should we keep on riding, Corey, or do you think that we should give the ponies a rest?' Making it clear, I thought, that in her mind I was the boss of this little outfit.

Andy, damn him, was grinning. 'We've got enough of a lead on them. Let's make night camp — no fire.'

We walked our horses ahead a mile or so to be away from the wolf carrion and the predators it would attract, unsaddled and blanketed up, all of us uncomfortable, cold and feeling a little helpless. The land was vast and we had cut our ties with any support we might have expected.

Eva sobbed for a little while as I tried to sleep. Maybe she was thinking about the man she intended to meet in Denver. I don't know. I had my own problems. I hadn't asked either of these females to ride with me; I hadn't expected Andy to ride us down. Though I suppose I should have guessed that he would.

I yawned, I slept. It was in the hour before dawn that I saw Andy working his way toward Marly's bed.

He made me think, inconsequentially, of one of those slinking prairie wolves. Silent, treacherous and deadly. I dragged my Colt into my left hand, an uncomfortable position, sat up and growled a warning:

'You touch her and I'll shoot, Andy.'

He smiled, but it was not pleasant. Hatless, he walked to my bed and hovered over me. The youthful cheerfulness was not there in his eyes, around the corners of his mouth.

'You can't mean what you said, Keogh,' he said in a low, warning voice.

'I meant it.'

'What's the girl to you?' he asked, crouching down beside me.

'Nothing,' I said.

'That's right. Nothing. What you said

— I'll take that as a mistake. A misunderstanding between friends. We will leave it at that, forget it.'

'If you harm her, Andy, I will be on you.' I was angry, determined and, yes, afraid at once. But I meant what I was saying.

'Are you going to gun me down with that left-handed draw of yours!' Andy laughed. 'I don't think you could hit a kitchen wall if you were locked inside the room.'

'That doesn't matter, Andy,' I said carefully. 'My hand is broken up, but if you were to touch that girl I would come after you. With elbows, knees, skull and teeth if I have to. I'm telling you . . . leave her alone.'

Andy laughed. 'Why, sure, partner! I didn't know she meant that much to you. I don't need any woman that bad.' He bent lower and his voice took on a menacing tone, 'Remember this, Keogh — we will always be friends. But if you ever cross me again, I will shoot you dead.'

He meant it. I could tell that he did. I did not sleep the remainder of the night, and rose early as the low sun burnished the mountain peaks and silvered the dew-heavy grass.

Andy was gone.

None of us was surprised, though there was not the relief we should have felt.

Marley asked me, 'What will he do?'

'Andy? He'll find the next town, the next woman, and forget us all within a week.' That was what I told her, although I did not believe it myself. Andy Givens was not a man to be scorned, and he would believe now that not only had the women turned their backs on his advances but that his best friend had sided with them.

I could do nothing about that. The land before us now began to rise and shape itself into folded hills, cut here and there with deep washes where freshets roared past through the pines and the Rockies loomed magnificently higher every morning. The nights were bitterly cold and without provisions other than the occasional game I could bring down with my awkward, left-handed shots, we began to suffer unimaginably. I will give the women this: they did not complain. Eva and Marly both knew that none of this was my fault. Had it been up to me, I would have just turned my pony's head southward and tried to find some warm pastures in New Mexico Territory to winter out on.

But day after day, Marly reminded me that it was all-important that Eva reach Denver where her true love was waiting for her. Both women were beginning to wear down now as we continued our brutal trek day after day. We had followed the Arkansas River until it fell away from our line of travel, skirted Bent's Old Fort and continued on, the land rising higher and higher. Eva resembled a mere sketch of a woman, a simulacrum, her head bobbing as she clung to the saddle horn hour after hour, determined to reach her goal.

'I never understood a part of this, back there in Tulip, I mean,' I said to Marly as we traversed a lengthy spread of broken knolls. 'I thought that Eva and Bull Mosely were . . . '

'That is what Bull thought,' Marly told me. 'The truth is that Eva never encouraged Bull. He was just another man — like Andy — who was dazzled by her looks and believed that he could own her.'

'It's too bad Eva can't find a way to make her intentions plainer to men,' I said sullenly.

'She can't help it!' Marly snapped. 'She is that way — friendly and open and men take it wrong. All of you . . . ' she ended on a critical note. I couldn't think of an answer, so I let the miles pass in uncompanionable silence. The pine trees and cedars were beginning to grow more thickly around us, clotted with scolding blue jays and raucous crows, red squirrels bounding from bough to bough.

'You are obviously devoted to your sister,' I ventured to Marly as we waded our horses across a tiny, quick-running rill. 'But what about you? Where is this all leading you?'

'It does not matter,' Marly said with an indifferent flip of her hand. 'Eva is the promise of our family. The pretty one, the clever one.'

'I see. Is that what you were always told?'

'It's clear, isn't it?' Marly asked. Her mouth, a lovely mouth I thought, grew tighter.

'How old are you, Marly?'

'Eighteen. What does that matter?'

'It doesn't matter. Except that you should be considering where your own life is leading you now.'

Marly fell into a deep silence which lasted for a mile or so. When she was herself again she began to explain a little more about the two of them.

'Father did not return from the War, Corey. Our mother used to pray all night for his homecoming. She left a lantern burning in the window for a full ten years after the surrender was signed at Appomattox. She became . . . not a mother, but a ghost among us living in a shadowy past. Eva and I ventured West. A man named Copperfield somehow remembered Eva from home — in Virginia — and he posted a letter to her. It was a very sweet, quite sad, lonely letter. I read it, of course. We had nothing left at home; Mother had lost her mind, you see. As young girls we did not know, but . . . that is not important. We came West, my sister and I, and have been continuing and continuing West. And there is just no end to it!'

She didn't cry, but it was close.

'My sister, you see,' Marly continued, 'is too much like my mother. She is not strong for all of her seeming confidence. She was content to sit at the window and only watch and wait for some white knight to appear. She must have read Copperfield's letter a hundred times, but she was so frightened of uprooting herself even though all of our small world was slowly dying around us! Afraid to undertake the journey. The vast expanse of the land out here is so daunting!'

'And so you took her by the hand and made her decision for her.'

'Something like that,' Marly replied. 'Eva became ill along the way and so we laid over for a few weeks in Tulip. By the time she had gotten well, she had already become the belle of the town. But with this business concerning Bull Mosely, I knew we had to be traveling on again. Eva needs a quiet, settled life somewhere, and Denver may be the answer. This Copperfield seems to be the sort who can make her content.'

'But for you, what is there in Denver? You are still only eighteen and quite alone,' I commented. Marly ignored my question, looking away.

'Copperfield will be a good man and true. I know this. And Eva will be happy . . . ' Then Marly did bow her head and cry. I remained silent, watching the far country.

★ ★ ★

It was on the sixteenth of October — I know this because the man we asked for directions kept a calendar — that we entered the town of Pueblo, Colorado. Marly, a little slyly, told Eva and me that she had enough silver money secreted inside her garments to provide us all with a real hotel bed and a hot bath. She was a woman, this Marly, despite her years.

Stabling the horses, I looked first for familiar ponies, scanned the main street for Andy's appaloosa or a body of men who might have been from the Tulip mob, even the Pocono Ranch hands. It seemed, fortunately, that we had left all and sundry far behind.

I had a bath.

For the many of you who have not gone weeks on the trail without being washed, I can't describe what that means. A rare luxury. Steam rising from the copper tub in peaceful, soothing waves. The bay rum scent from the barber's shop beyond the door, also quite soothing in its way.

Friend, I could have died happily soaking in that tub.

Then I got up out of it, toweled off and had to start worrying about the women again.

The simple truth was that I still had no idea what to do with the two of them. We were a long way from Denver, broke-down and plain broke. Busted. Whatever change Marly had scrounged to pay for our hotel rooms was now gone. So here we sat again without provisions and three trail-beaten ponies to our names.

Nevertheless, now bathed, barbered and shaved, I felt nearly ten feet tall as I strode down the plankwalk toward the hotel. The sun was bright, the day clear — my right hand even seemed to be regaining some of its former flexibility.

At the door to the hotel Marly waited. She looked as pretty as a picture. Somehow she had found a place to get her blue dress washed and pressed. There was a tiny blue ribbon in her dark hair, and — I had to notice — there were a few appealing curves beneath the lace bodice of the dress that I hadn't observed before. It was all too good to last.

'He's here,' Marley said breathlessly.

'Who?' I glanced around. 'Andy?' I didn't expect him to show up in our tracks, but it wouldn't have surprised me either.

'No!' Marley said, gripping both of my wrists until I shifted the injured one away. 'I mean Bull Mosely. He'll kill one of us for sure.'

'Not me,' I said, trying to make light of matters. 'I've done nothing to the man.'

'But — ' Marley began hesitantly. 'He wants Andy Givens, and you're the closest thing to him that he can find. Mosely will blame you for stealing Eva away from him. He feels the need to vent his fury, and you are the likely target.'

I didn't like her logic, but I had to admit that she was right. You are always judged by the company that you keep, are you not? And my old saddle companion was not one I chose to be judged by. Marley was not finished.

'And we don't know what Mosely might do to Eva once he's on the prod!' She asked me, her eyes pleading: 'Corey, what are we going to do?'

Run was the first answer that rose to my lips, but we had three exhausted mounts and nowhere to hide on the open plains.

'I guess I'll have to face him down, Marley. Maybe things aren't as bad as they seem,' I replied wearily.

'But they are, Corey. They are!'

Yes, they were, I had to agree. But what else was there to do? I returned to the white-hot streets to find Bull Mosely and confront him.

5

There was smoke billowing out of the saloon doors, and the rising sun prodded an answering mist from the long-grass plains. I felt like a doomed man walking through a world of smoke and shadows. Me, with my right hand so battered that I hadn't even tried to use it on a fork yet and my awkward left-handed holster slung loosely on my hip. I understood the look of concern in Marly's eyes as I had walked away from her, for there was really nothing I could do against the monster Bull Mosely except to try to explain things reasonably.

Bull Mosely had not as yet seemed to be an overly-reasonable man.

I trudged the narrow, white-dust street knowing that I could find Bull without much effort. Strangers in a new town seldom wander far from the main thoroughfare where provisions and such could be found. I looked down at myself. My newly barbered confidence had faded. Here I was a beat-up saddle tramp with a wrong-sided gun and a busted-up hand. I couldn't frighten a schoolboy.

I wondered, disheartenedly, if Andy Givens's taunts hadn't been well-directed. Maybe I could not take care of myself . . .

Or anyone else. Fearful, Marly's eyes had still shown a trust in my ability to take care of her and her sister. It was a trust that was probably misplaced.

They grabbed me as I crossed in front of the alley mouth.

There were three, but it felt like six. I went down in a jumble, having no chance to fight them off. Bull Mosely stood hovering over me, blocking out the sun, his bear-paw fists bunched ominously.

'Where is she?' he demanded.

'Who?' I asked and he kicked me savagely in the ribs. One of the sodbusters with him laughed.

'I won't ask you again!' Bull threatened.

'Then don't,' I replied, curling up in a defensive ball. I had a brief moment's satisfaction from my clever retort before Bull kicked me again. A kick? Well, it was more like a pile-driver impacting against my ribs. I heard something crack; I could not draw a breath properly. I regretted my remark. I regretted Bull Mosely and Tulip, Andy Givens and the general population of the planet.

I knew he was going to kick me to death. I knew I could not tell him where Eva was hiding from him.

'Do your best,' I managed to mutter through lips that felt paralyzed, and Bull did it. One more brutally sharp kick that seemed to echo through my brain and somehow numbed the earlier pain. I was too close to blacking out to experience pain any longer. I heard one of the other men tell Bull in a hiss:

'You'll kill him! This isn't Tulip, Bull! We'll have the law down on us if you don't hold off.'

Bull Mosely backed away, panting like a great, troubled animal.

'I'll see you again, saddle tramp. You know I will!'

I did, too. As I lay shivering, drawn up into a ball for protection, there was no doubt in my mind that given the chance this man would do further damage to my body. I heard sounds of urging, of muttered curses as the three sod-busters briefly huddled together indecisively.

'Bull, we've got to go,' the more cautious of the farmers told Mosely again. 'This ain't our town.'

'All right,' Mosely rumbled. 'What I'd like to do is cut his ears off, though.' He started away, then I heard the heavy footsteps return. 'Here's one to remember me by,' Bull said.

I had been trying to rise and caught in the awkward position that I was, I could not even roll away as he smashed the heel of his boot down against my left hand.

Enough was enough. I couldn't curse, cry, fight or run. I simply lay face down in the dusty alley whimpering like an injured pup, contemplating through the pain what sort of life might await a man with two broken hands in this hard country.

I lay still for an hour, an eternity. Motion, any motion, shot savage pain through my hammering skull. I knew I had at least one broken rib. My left hand and right hand dueled for the honor of hurting the most. There was blood in my mouth. I didn't remember anyone hitting me, but I suppose one of them must have as they first swarmed over me. The day was cool, the sun as hot as a branding iron on my back. When I felt, rather than saw, the shadow cross my face I could only sob like a child. The man stood over me and I waited for the next blow to fall.

'How many times do I have to tell you before you believe me, Keogh? Old son, you just cannot get along without me.'

It was Andy Givens. He was crouched down beside me, hat tilted back.

I swear he was smiling.

'How bad does it hurt, Keogh?' he asked.

'Pretty bad, Andy. Real bad. Worse than when that old brindle longhorn steer trampled me down.'

'It looked like they were doing a pretty good job of it,' Andy said. 'Let's at least sit you up.'

He hooked his hands under my arms and tugged, twisting me around so that I was braced against the sun-warmed plank wall of the building beside the alley. There were tears in my eyes, blood leaking from my nose and drying on my chin. My rib was throbbing with pain. Both of my hands were shot. My shirt was torn, my jeans out at the knee. I sat, hands cupped on my lap, looking up out of the bright yellow light of day at the shadowed face of Andy Givens, remembering what he had just said.

'You saw them!' My voice was hoarse. I had to turn my head to spit out some blood. 'You said you saw them beating me, Andy. And you did nothing to stop it?'

Andy laughed. 'I didn't want to start shooting in a strange town.'

I didn't have the energy to sustain a true rage. I simply sat there, crumpled and battered, staring up at my old friend. A memory of a friend. He wouldn't have had to shoot Mosely or one of the others. He could simply have flashed his Colt and they would have backed off quick enough.

I couldn't quite read the light in his eyes, shadowed as they were by the brim of his hat. But I knew that I had fallen out of favor, that I had crossed Andy — in his mind — back along the trail. There was a fierce anger in me now. I believe that if I could have found my gun, managed to cock and fire with my broken hands, I would have shot him. To have a friend, a saddle partner stand and watch as I was beat half to death and do nothing . . . I closed my eyes and shook my head heavily.

'Let's get you up on your feet,' Andy said. I felt his hand on my arm again. 'Then tell me where the women are sheltered up, and I'll get you over there.'

I opened my eyes again. 'No,' I told him definitely.

'What do you mean?' Andy asked, with true surprise. 'Do you want to sit here in the alley and die?'

'Maybe,' I answered. 'Maybe I don't care anymore.'

'You're delirious, Keogh! Crazy with the hurt.'

'Probably,' I agreed. 'You don't understand, do you. I will *not* take you to where the girls are staying. You're not thinking of me. If you were, you would have stopped those sodbusters from beating me half to death. You're still thinking only of yourself. You're no different than Bull Mosely. No better at all.'

I had my arm hooked around my

damaged ribcage. The breath wasn't coming easy. There was sharp, jagged pain inside. I recalled Eva's words.

'Eva said,' I panted, 'that you were *all* trouble, Andy. I've forgiven a lot of it. I'd say to myself, 'Well, that's just Andy being Andy!' And we were, after all, partners. But Eva got it wrong, Andy. Something has happened to you — I don't know what it is; I'm not smart enough to figure it out. But it's not just that you are trouble . . .

'You've gone bad, Andy! There's no saving grace in you. You are plain bad, worse than Bull Mosely could figure to be. He at least,' I said with my breathing becoming still more ragged, 'he believes in that granite skull of his that he is on some righteous mission, that he loves Eva and she's been stolen away from him. You — ' I paused to cough up some blood from my bad lungs. 'Andy, you don't even have that simple-minded excuse. You don't care for Eva. Only for Andy Givens.'

Andy was standing up straight,

peering toward the head of the alleyway. After a moment's reflection he whispered harshly, 'I could just kick you a few more times, Keogh. I could finish you off good and proper, couldn't I? Who would know?'

'No one,' I said, spitting blood.

'I want to know where you have those girls stashed,' Andy demanded, bending over me. Now I could see his eyes. They had an ugly glint in them. Nothing remained of the man I had ridden with and thought I had known. Nothing at all.

'No, Andy. No, I won't tell you.'

For just a moment his face grew even tighter and his eyes, pale as they were, grew dark. Just for a moment his hand flickered near the grips of his Colt.

Then I saw him shrug and heard him laugh.

'To hell with you then!' he said. Then Andy turned away and started down the alley, his thumbs hooked carelessly into his belt, his walk swaggering.

And I swear I heard him whistling softly.

I sat there long enough to draw attention. A large shaggy spotted dog came along, slinked up to me, muttered a questioning growl. Then it licked my face until I waved it away. I had to move. Move before the local law showed up and threw me in jail — had that telegraph wire carried my description into Pueblo? Move before Bull Mosely convinced himself that it was a good idea to come back and kick me a few more times for the fun of it . . .

Before Andy Givens could decide that he might as well return and finish me off.

Before either of them could find Eva Pierce.

And Marly!

That was what finally gave me the impetus to drag myself upright. I would regret it all my life if these men got to Eva Pierce, but I could not live with myself if I let anything happen to Marly. Did that mean that I was in . . . ?

I shook away the foolish thought, could not continue the unspoken sentence. Truthfully, I was not even able to frame the question. My thoughts were crowded and pain-blunted, bloody and confused.

One thing at a time, Keogh! I thought with a sternness that did not immediately translate to action. I had to get on my feet. That was first. Then . . . *no, get to your feet first, Keogh. Any other decision can follow later.*

Rise. How was that done? Twist, brace both broken hands against the hot wall, draw knees up . . . that was wrong. Could not be done. The heavy confusion continued to fog my every thought and plan. The shaggy dog had returned with something dead in its mouth to show me.

I rose.

I saw the glint of steel against the alley floor, managed to bend over and scoop up my Colt and shove it awkwardly away in its holster. That accomplished, I leaned against the side of the building, taking a series of short, painful breaths and staggered on drunkenly. Marly would be worried about me.

'Hey, put the bottle away and get out of the sun!' someone yelled at me as I wove my way toward the hotel. Laughter followed. I paid it no mind. I didn't know what I looked like, but I knew I wasn't a pretty sight.

I was beginning to have moments close to clarity, and I wove away from the hotel, angling toward the stable where we had put our ponies up. Beside the two-story structure was a water barrel. I stumbled toward it and washed my face in what smelled more like brine than water. Probably the barrel had been used to catch run-off from the last rain which might have been weeks ago in this country. Yet I managed to wash most of the blood away, wipe my hair back with damp fingers, and after another minute spent leaning against the plank wall of the stable, staring at my scuffed boots, I managed to draw myself erect and walk to the front of the building.

I found two men inside the dark, horse-smelling building, one a huge man with a black beard who nevertheless had no menace about him. The other was a scrawny red-headed youth with a rake in his hand who paid no attention at all to me.

The man with the black beard looked me over, top to toe and grinned affably. 'Who won the scrap, partner?'

'Definitely not me,' I said, trying to force a smile with my bruised mouth. 'I've got some business I want to discuss with you.'

'All right,' he said, 'I'm always ready to talk business. Come on into this little cubbyhole I call my office, and tell me what you have in mind.'

I explained: 'Yesterday we stabled up three ponies here. We lack the funds to keep them grained for as long as they need. And the two ladies have expressed a desire to proceed to Denver by stagecoach.' I leaned forward across the tiny scarred desk where a few record books lay scattered. 'I'd like to sell you those horses, if you're agreeable.'

The bearded man leaned back and scratched as his hidden chin. 'Those ponies have been ridden a long way.'

'Yes, sir.'

'Gaunted out pretty much.'

'Yes, sir.'

He folded his thick arms and closed his eyes thoughtfully before suddenly bellowing:

'Virgil!'

In a moment the stable-hand appeared. 'The kid,' the black-bearded man explained, 'is only half-bright, but he knows more about horses than you or I ever will. He nearly lives among them. Virgil,' he said, 'are you familiar with the three horses this man brought in yesterday? Him and two women?' Briefly he described our mounts as the vacant-eyed Virgil listened.

'Yes, Clive,' Virgil said. 'I recollect.'

'How would you rate them?' the

black-bearded man asked.

'Game but not lame. No heat in the hocks . . . can I get back to my chores now, Clive?'

The stable owner smiled indulgently and waved his hired hand away. Leaning nearer to me he said, 'I can't give you top-dollar, friend. Times are tough in this town. But I believe that I can let you have enough to pay for passage to Denver on the coach and take care of the ladies' needs for awhile.'

'That's all I'm asking,' I said.

I suppose I'm a poor horse-trader on top of everything else, but we were in dire need of cash money just then. My thinking was that our nags were pretty beat-down and the women were almost as bushed. Me, I couldn't hook a saddle over my roan if I had to. I wasn't sure I could even handle the reins right now, the state my hands were in.

Besides, instead of riding into the higher mountains with me — a crippled saddle tramp as their only guide, Eva and Marly would at least have the added protection of a stage driver and the man riding shotgun-guard along with any other passengers who might be on the coach. I should be able to get them to Denver . . . so long as nothing else went horribly wrong.

'Are you meaning to throw those saddles in on the deal, seeing that you'll have no use for them?' the stable owner asked as he reached into a lower drawer for his cashbox, on top of which, I noticed, was a heavy revolver. 'Clive' was not trying to cheat me, but he was in the business of making a living.

'I suppose so,' I said with a sigh. A man hates to give up his saddle, but it really was of no use to me just then.

'One of them's a side-saddle,' Clive said, with a shake of his head, 'it's not often we get a call for one.' I had begun to tremble. I was unsteady on my feet and my ribs and hands were throbbing with pain. I wasn't up to dickering with the man.

'The whole bunch — horses and tack.

Give me what you think is fair,' I said.

I thought of the times all of us line-riders had been short-changed on our wages here and there. Clive was no thief, but he was cutting himself a good deal, I knew. I just never had any luck when it came to money. It was always desperate times, it seemed, when a man took what he could get. And so I did now.

'Where's the stage station?' I asked.

'Up about half a mile, but they can take your fare in that restaurant across the street. Stage always lets the passengers stop and eat there.'

Emerging again into the bright sunlight I paused, holding my ribs. Peering up and down the street I saw no one familiar and so I took a chance and staggered across the street toward the hotel where Eva and Marly would be waiting. The narrow-built desk clerk glanced at me with disapproval, but said nothing. He had seen worse than me pass through the door in his time, I figured.

'Is there a back way out of here?' I asked him and his eyes narrowed as if I was thinking of stiffing him on the bill. To allay that suspicion, I splashed some coins on the counter and asked him to settle our tab. He became more talkative as he tallied the bill, offering to itemize the receipt for me. I waved that off, it being of no use to me, but found out where the back entrance was. My plan — such as it was — seemed to be shaping up. Before starting up the stairs to Marly's room, I slipped the man some extra silver and told him:

'If *anyone* shows up asking about the ladies, you just say that they've checked out, understand?'

He gave me a sly, uncalled-for wink and scooped the silver change into his purse.

I found Marly at the door to her room, waiting for me. She looked me over, gave a muffled gasp and urged me inside, closing the door behind us.

'Sit down on the bed, for God's sake,

Corey! I'll have them send up some hot water.'

'No,' I said, though I did sag on to her unmade bed. 'We are going to be out of here in five minutes. Throw together whatever you have to take. Tell Eva to do the same.'

But Eva had already appeared in the doorway connecting the two rooms. Her gasp was more audible than Marly's had been. Her hands went to her mouth and for a moment I thought she was going to scream or cry out.

'What happened! Is Mosely in town?' She asked fearfully.

'I'll explain later,' I said insistently. 'For now, get ready to leave.'

'How can we . . . our poor horses . . . ' Eva was suddenly in a panic.

'I sold the horses,' I told them. I bent over, finding it harder yet to breathe, clutching my ribs tightly. 'We're taking the next stagecoach out of town.'

Marly had begun throwing her poor belongings into the canvas bag she had carried. Eva continued to be swamped by bewilderment, making no move to comply.

'My beautiful little pony? Why did you sell it, Corey? And what has happened to you? I don't understand this at all!'

'Later,' I kept saying. 'Later, I'll tell you all about it later.'

'A stagecoach?' Eva could not be stilled. 'Where are we going now? Corey, where are you taking us!'

'To Denver, Eva. On to Denver. Mr Copperfield will be waiting for you there.'

6

The back exit from the hotel led out on to a second-floor landing and then down a flight of wooden steps to the alley behind the building. I eyed the foot of the landing cautiously. I was beginning to be wary of any and all alleys. I started down, leading Eva and Marley with their small bundles of belongings.

Marley had had time to bathe my face with cold soapy water while we waited for her sister to collect her goods. Still my face was puffed and would soon discolor. My ribs ached wretchedly. We had flexed and probed the fingers of my left hand and found that it had not been nearly so horribly damaged as my right hand. I even believed that if trouble came I would be able to fire my revolver with my left as well as I had before. Which was not that good at all. Certainly not good enough against a man like Andy Givens.

Like some sort of misshapen, hobbling school-master I herded the women through the oily, trash-cluttered alleys toward the restaurant, explaining a little of my plan as we went.

'I was told that we can pay our fares in the restaurant office. I don't know what time the next coach pulls in — Clive couldn't tell me. We'll just have to hide out in the restaurant until departure time. Neither Mosely nor Andy will be able to do us any mischief — even if they do find us while we're among the crowd in there.

'Then we'll be on board the stage and they'll try halting it at their own risk. There will be a shotgun rider, and those men don't hesitate to use force if anyone tries to stop their coaches.'

Marly nodded and continued along beside me, determined and deliberate in her stride. Eva, on the other hand, dragged her heels, looked frequently over her shoulder for any pursuers, asked me dozens of questions which I just did not feel up to answering. My breathing around those cracked ribs was getting no less painful. I knew it would be awhile before they healed. I had been kicked by a horse once and all the doctor knew to do was shake his head and bind my ribs up as tight as possible.

We entered the restaurant by the back door, startling the pair of big-bellied cooks at their labors, passed through the kitchen and were given seats at the table farthest from the front entrance. It was the best spot we could have found, and I didn't blame the waitress for offering it to us. The way I looked, it's a wonder she didn't ask me to eat out back with the dogs. In deference to the ladies, however, they allowed me to sit among the civilized people.

I held my head in my hands, elbows on the table while people murmured around us. I left the ordering to Marly, and it didn't take long before coffee and biscuits with honey began to appear on the tabletop. Marly touched my arm.

'Maybe I could slip out and get you a clean shirt, at least,' she whispered.

'And risk running into Andy Givens.' I wagged my head. 'No. That's a bad idea. I'm all right. I've looked like a fool before!' I said. And I felt like one now, roughed-up as I was, but the people around us were polite enough to pretend not to notice my condition, and when breakfast began to arrive — ham, eggs, fried potatoes, I forgot my troubles long enough to fill up my stomach.

Later, I made my way to the front desk and asked about coach fares. The man there was busy with some sort of business papers and he just tapped a finger on the yellowed schedule of prices hanging on the wall beside him. When he was finished with what he was doing I paid for three through-fares to Denver, got three big red tickets which I tucked away in my torn shirt and made my way back to the table.

'It should be about a two-hour wait,' I told the ladies. 'The worst is behind us now.'

I didn't really believe it, though I smiled at Marley trying to reassure her. She saw the concern in my eyes but said nothing. The trouble was that Bull Mosely was still crazy with what he took for love and would not stop following after Eva, despite what I had told the women.

The bigger problem — I realized this now — was that Andy Givens was just plain crazy and there was no predicting what he would do or how violent he might become in his own strange pursuits.

We sat and we waited. And waited. People came, ate their meals and left as we sat watching the front door for any sight of Mosely and his crew or for Andy Givens. We drank coffee and waited as the brass-bound clock on the wall behind us ticked time slowly away. The waitress obviously wanted us to clear out of the restaurant so that the table could be used by someone else. I went ahead and paid our bill, giving the woman a large tip which only mollified her a little. There were whispered conversations among the staff watching us. Eva and Marley both became nervous, fidgety.

'They don't want us here,' Marley whispered to me.

'I know that, but we're staying.'

Time moved slowly, plodding past, but after another hour I heard a different sort of conversation around us, and glancing up I saw a new group of people — three of them — entering the restaurant, their faces excited, their eyes weary, their clothes dusty with travel.

'The stagecoach must have pulled in,' I told the two women. 'Have a look.'

Marley glanced around at the new-comers and smiled hopefully at me.

Eva asked, 'Why don't we get aboard, if we're going?'

'They'll be changing horses at the stage stop while the passengers eat. We watch. When the driver returns to call for them, we go with them.'

It seemed an eternity. I thought I had never seen people eat so slowly as these stagecoach passengers, although that was my imagination. I wanted out of there, away from Pueblo, from the hunting men. There was a prosperous-looking big man among the travelers, and when he would pause between bites to speak, I mentally urged him to shut up and eat!

After half an hour a rough-looking man with a short red beard poked his head into the room and called in, 'Denver stage is pulling out in five minutes, folks!'

Eva started to rise, but I put my hand on her arm. 'Wait until they're all ready to leave. We want to go in a bunch with them.'

'But surely . . . ' Eva complained in exasperation.

'But surely nothing,' I told her more sharply than I had intended. 'I won't take another beating. And if you want to see Denver and Mr Copperfield, we do everything we can to ensure our safety. Do you understand, Eva?'

Eva nodded meekly.

After a time Marly said quietly to me, 'It's just that she's afraid, Corey. Eager and afraid.'

'I know. I'm sorry. But we can't take any more chances.' Briefly, too briefly, Marly's fingers touched the back of my hand indicating that she understood. The stagecoach driver had reappeared at the entrance.

'Coach to Denver is leaving, folks!' And we rose to join the rest of the travelers, sensing safety and freedom from pursuit.

My left hand did not drift far from my holstered Colt as we stepped out of the restaurant stage-stop into the morning sunlight. I saw no one I did not wish to see as we clambered aboard. The stage had a strangely mismatched team: three stolid bay horses and one wild-eyed piebald on the off-wheel. I didn't care just then if they were four mules or goats! We were on our way.

The red-bearded driver looked competent with his long, fringed gauntlets, the shotgun rider had the kind of tough, pale-blue eyes that look right through a man.

There were three other passengers seated opposite us as we squeezed into the cramped quarters of the Butterfield stage: the prosperous-looking man I had noted earlier; a matronly woman named Revere who, as we were soon to discover, could not stop talking about her daughter and her new son-in-law, an army captain; and a sallow, unfriendly middle-aged man with a lean jaw and a Remington pistol carried high on his waist. His presence too, I found reassuring.

The driver whooped and his bullwhip cracked above the horses' ears and the stage lurched into motion. I leaned back thankfully against the hard seat between Eva and Marly. I was hatless, battered, my shirt and jeans torn. I wore my gun on the wrong side of my hips and I knew my face showed recent cuts and bruising. I caught our new fellow travelers eyeing me with puzzlement and concern. I could not have cared less.

Marly was close beside me and it seemed that somehow I had managed to salvage the disastrous situation.

The stage rocked on for mile after mile across the long-grass, oak-studded land as we continued to climb toward Denver. The driver knew his task well and so did his team of horses, apparently. Eva fell into a conversation with the prosperous traveler in the pearl-gray suit, Warren Travers by name. He, it seemed, was part owner of a Comstock Lode mine which had done well, especially in silver. I barely listened. To me the rough riding coach was more comfortable than any of the others could have guessed. With Marly next to me, the occasional touch of her concerned hand on my still-swollen right wrist, my stomach full for the first time in awhile, our troubles apparently left behind, I was content.

I even managed to doze for a time. The sun began to heel over toward the west. The driver of the coach shouted out something that I didn't catch, but the mine-owner repeated it to us.

'The next stage stop is Canyon City. We'll be there in about an hour,' he said with the confident knowledge of an experienced traveler. 'The food is not so good as that in Pueblo, but there is always plenty of it!'

He leaned back, glancing at the gold watch he wore on a chain across his ample belly. The sallow man with the tight expression still had said not a word. The garrulous matron, Mrs. Revere, continued to prattle on about her daughter and how fine a catch Captain Mason had been, how happy they would be to see her.

Marly touched my shoulder and whispered, 'It will all be all right now, Corey. Thanks to you.'

I could only hope she was right.

I had not forgotten that there was a

man with a strange compulsive madness behind us on the Colorado trail.

Sundown found us at a remote stage-stop. Built of adobe blocks, sheltered beneath a grove of live-oak trees, lantern-light shone in its windows and smoke curled up from the chimney into the darkening sky, promising warmth and comfort.

Inside the low-ceilinged building we were met by a birdlike woman who bounced from point to point, setting dishes, coffee pots and bread on the two plank tables and a phlegmatic man I took to be her husband who rose once, shook hands with the mine owner and the sallow traveler and planted himself again firmly in his leather-bottomed chair.

The three women were led off to some sheltered room to clean up. I sat the end of one of the plank tables, waiting for them to return. The mine owner, Warren Travers, was in close conversation with the manager of the stage stop. Not much was said, but it ended with both men laughing out loud over some private comment.

Smoke from the fire backed up into the room when the wind gusted, not enough to make it unpleasant, but the scent of burning cedar wood pervaded the place. The stage driver and his shotgun rider had still not come in from the stables and so we waited for our meal. Opposite me, seated at the second table, the expressionless sallow man studied me closely. I still hadn't heard him exchange a word with anyone. His eyes were intense, his mouth pursed. I saw him lean back, fumble in his shirt for a cigar.

And with that gesture he spread his jacket enough for me to catch the glint of a silver star pinned to his shirt front. I cursed silently and tried my best to look both uninterested and innocent. No wonder the man had been eyeing me so narrowly. Wretch that I was, I looked like someone who might have been up to no good, perhaps making my escape from the law.

Which I was, I considered dejectedly.

There was the small matter of a man's murder back in Tulip.

The three women re-entered the room at that moment, disengaging the lawman's eyes. He rose as Mrs. Revere seated herself opposite him at that table. Eva and Marly swept in behind her and took their seats, Marly next to me, Eva across from her sister. Within the next minute as if they knew from past experience that supper was ready to be served, the driver and shotgun guard opened the heavy oaken door and entered after stamping their boots to shake off the red clay they had accumulated in the yard. Both had rinsed off and wiped their hair back with water.

Between them they carried a heavy lock-box, and crossing the room they spoke to the man with the badge.

'Where do you want this, Blair?'

'Back room,' the lawman answered. 'You know where I sleep.' As he said this, he kept his eyes fixed on me. I

119

looked away deliberately.

With everyone settled at the tables, the birdlike woman whom her husband called Jane began serving large platters of food-steak and fried potatoes, baked apples. The conversation among those at the opposite table lowered to a contented murmur. At our table there was near silence. Eva and Marly exchanged some small talk about the food and their weariness, but I was not in the mood for any conversation. Marly was observant enough to see that I was troubled again, and asked me with a signal of her hand. I leaned toward her and whispered:

'The smaller man traveling with us — he's a lawman of some sort. Probably a line detective.'

'Oh,' was all Marly said, but I now saw her eyes flicker to the yellow-faced man from time to time.

'We're staying the night here,' Eva said to me. 'Did you know that?'

I had not, although I should have guessed. It would be unwise for the stage company to run their coaches through the night, risking injury to their horses and subsequently to the passengers. If a horse did go down, even if there were no injuries, being stranded at night in the cold mountains would be more than uncomfortable.

'At least we'll have warm, safe accommodations for tonight,' Eva was saying. Her face had brightened and her old smile appeared again. 'And Mrs. Revere says that our schedule has us arriving in Denver at noonday tomorrow. So Corey, don't look so worried, you have done it! Our journey is nearly at an end.'

I wasn't so sure. That night I shared a small room with the red-haired stage driver, whom I had only heard called 'Allie', who was not much for conversation, thankfully, and with Mr Travers who finally yawned himself to sleep after an explanation of some mining technique I did not understand and Allie was utterly uninterested in. I lay awake, watching the starlight through the high, slit window of the room, and considered.

The stage line might rest their ponies and balk at running them in darkness, but if there were pursuing men on the trail behind this, they would not be so cautious. They could easily catch up with us overnight. It would make no sense to assault a tightly-constructed outpost directly, where half a dozen armed men could easily fight them off. If it were me, I thought, I would think this over and realize that there were other ways to attempt their objective.

For example, the horses could be scattered, leaving all inside stranded. Again such a risk seemed unreasonable . . . for sane men. I tossed restlessly on my bunk. Unsleeping still, I wondered how long Bull Mosely would pursue his runaway lover. It seemed unlikely that his farmer friends would be willing to go along with such a mad scheme for the sake of his unrequited love.

Andy . . . yes, he was capable of such a wild scheme, but he was a lone rider, was he not? What could he do by himself? I frowned deeply, wondering. Maybe he was not alone any longer. He might have gathered some men desperate enough to follow him. He could even have somehow induced Bull Mosely to accompany him, as wild an idea as that seemed. How could that be done?

Suppose Andy had promised Bull to help him retrieve Eva if Andy could have Marly? It seemed absurd on the surface. Even Andy would not go that far for revenge, for a woman, for . . . I and then it struck me.

For gold? Yes. I knew Andy's thieving ways, remembered him talking about the banks in Denver. Those, however, were formidable brick structures with steel-doored safes. Why wait for the gold to reach Denver?

The strong-box I had seen earlier, the presence of the accompanying lawman . . . the stage was carrying gold! I might have guessed it earlier, but my mind had been in a fog since the beating I had taken from Mosely. But how could Andy know this, assuming it was so?

Simple. I had seldom met anyone as garrulous as my wealthy sleeping neighbor, Warren Travers, and if anyone would know what the stage was carrying, it would be the self-important mine boss.

Perhaps my night thoughts were running wild, my fear giving my inventions reality only in my own mind. Still I did not sleep as the long night rolled over. I wondered if I should speak to the man with the badge, Blair, in the morning. And tell him what? He was suspicious enough of me as it was. Suppose he did think it over and decide that *I* could be the inside man on such an attempt, ready to fling open the door to the stage-stop to allow entry to the raiders if we were set upon?

Crazy! It was all crazy, I tried to convince myself. My imagination was over-active, my unfounded fears feeding upon themselves. Calming slowly, I rolled on to my side and having convinced myself that I was a child being visited by hobgoblins in the night, fell off at last to a troubled sleep.

I awoke early, the orange light of dawn glowing in the high slit window above my bed, marking a bright rectangle on the far wall. Travers slept soundly. Allie, the stage driver, was awake — I could tell from his movements — but in no hurry to rise from his warm blankets and face the chill of morning. With my blanket around my shoulders I sat on the edge of my bunk and tugged on my boots. Yawning, I scratched my head and looked back upon my night fears and smiled at my own vivid imaginings. Here was morning, quiet and calm, and this day held the promise of the end of the long trail. A man can be such a fool, I thought. It was then that a voice rang out from beyond the doorway.

'Fire! Everybody up. They've set fire to the station!'

7

I grabbed for my gunbelt, roused the heavily-sleeping Warren Travers and simultaneously realized that the wood-smoke I had taken as the preparation of a morning fire was much too heavy, the heat too intense.

The stage driver, Allie, fairly bounded from his bed, quickly alert for trouble. He snatched up his Winchester and asked me, 'What is it?'

'We're on fire.'

'Adobe doesn't burn!' he argued pointlessly as we started toward the door, half-towing the bewildered mine boss between us.

'It'll be the roof then. They'll have thrown fire-brands up there.'

'Who?' Allie shouted at me.

'How the hell should I know?' I yelled back. But I thought I knew.

When we reached the common room

the smoke was billowing inside. We could hear the roof of the stage station crackling with flame. Everyone was up and dressed: the threat of fire had brought them all instantly alert. I searched first for Marly, found her with her arm around Eva, both of them with their hair in a night tangle, both frightened, as they had the right to be.

'What are we standing around for!' the plump stationmaster shouted and he started for the door. I tried to grab his arm in passing and stop him, but failed. He flung open the front door and was shot down before he could cross the threshold.

'Damn all!' Blair rumbled. 'Everybody get against a wall, away from that door!' he told us.

'Who's out there?' Allie asked no one in particular. 'What do they want?'

We didn't have to wait long for an answer. As black smoke was drawn past us and out the open door, a familiar voice rang out from the oak trees across the yard.

'Whoever's in charge,' the voice of Andy Givens shouted, 'give us what we want or stay where you are and roast.'

Blair stepped nearer the door, gun in his hand and yelled back, 'Who is that! What do you want! We've women in here and — ' The sudden collapse of a section of roof near the back of the station interrupted the lawman. It came down with an explosive sound. Golden embers shot up from the burning beams.

'Send out the women!' Andy called back. 'Them and the strongbox. If you don't do it, and fast, we'll stand where we are and gun down any man trying to escape.'

'I won't go!' Mrs. Revere said, her voice a near-scream. Marly, who had recognized Andy's voice, calmed her.

'It's not you they want, Mrs. Revere. It's me and my sister. We'll go out if it will save the rest of you.' Marly was resolute. Eva clung to her sister's arm, shaking her head from side to side, her eyes wide. Marly shook her. 'We have to, Eva. It's that or burn to death in here and see the others lose their lives because of us.'

Blair, choking on the accumulating smoke, called out to Andy. 'The women say they'll come!'

'Fine,' Andy Givens said calmly. 'Them and the gold shipment. Then we let the rest of you come out.'

'I'll bring the strongbox to you!' Blair called. The sallow lawman seemed to have lost his nerve. I didn't blame him. With flames licking at the walls inside and a band of armed killers without, it was enough to panic anybody.

'Not you!' Andy shouted. 'Let Keogh bring it. Keogh! I know you're in there, you bring the strongbox.'

Blair glowered at me, his face firelit and angry. His eyes said it all — I was a member of the raiders' gang. He would have liked to shoot me down then and there, I thought. But he couldn't under the circumstances. Nor could I possibly carry the heavy strongbox, the shape my hands were in. I yelled out through the smoke.

'I can't carry the gold, Andy! My hands are too busted up!'

'Drag it, then, Keogh! Shuck your sidearm and then start dragging it out of there or watch everyone inside die!'

At the first demand Allie and the shotgun rider had carried the box out into the common room, ready themselves to turn it over. Someone else's gold in trade for their own lives made sense to the two stage company employees. Now, bending low, I took a grip on one of the strongbox's iron handles and dragged it past the dead way-station manager and out on to the porch, a cloud of black smoke swirling around me.

'Marly!' I shouted. 'Don't wait any longer. Come on!'

Heaving, I dragged the box down off the wooden porch and into the yard.

'Keep coming, Keogh! All the way over here,' Andy yelled from the oak grove.

I moved heavily, drawing a deep

groove in the soil. I saw Marly rush to me, hurrying Eva along. Marly gripped the other handle and we stumbled and staggered our way toward the cluster of oak trees. I saw Andy, smiling, step from behind the thick trunk of an old oak. I shouted at him.

'Here it is! Now let the others come out of there, Andy!'

'Just a little farther, Keogh. Get the strongbox behind these trees. Then I'll let them come.'

To the house he shouted: 'Start throwing your iron out, boys! I'll be counting guns. Then you can get out of there. When you come out, don't run this way. Head toward the corral.'

I stood panting, my chest heaving, my back against a tree. Marly was sheltering her sister in her arms.

'That wasn't so hard now, was it, Keogh?' Andy asked in a low voice. He lifted my chin with the barrel of his Winchester. We had heard the clatter of guns being thrown out on to the porch. Now Andy told his men:

'Let 'em come out, but keep your rifles on them.'

I glanced at the other faces around me. I should have known — Bull Mosely and his two friends. Somehow Andy had worked his charm on them and brought them over to his side. I supposed that Bull had been convinced that riding with Andy could get his Eva back, and his share of the gold — more than he could make in ten years on his farm — would allow him to take care of her in a manner that would make Eva overlook his other shortcomings as a potential mate.

Bull stood hovering near Eva and Marly, his dull eyes hungry, his jaw slack. The roar behind me caused me to turn my head. The roof of the stage station had completely collapsed. Fire, smoke and fans of sparks erupted into the morning air. I could make out the stumbling figures of the survivors huddled together near the empty corral, staring helplessly back at the wreckage of the burning building.

'Somebody's sure to see that,' Andy said as the smoke rose higher and plumed against the sky. 'Let's get moving.'

The desolate little group behind us could do nothing but watch us go. Their horses, of course, had been scattered. Andy was too shrewd not to leave them all afoot. They didn't dare make a move toward their guns. Andy was whistling as we made our way through the oaks. Following him were the two women and myself guarded by Bull Mosely. The other two sodbusters toting the strongbox between them followed.

Just beyond the trees stood the stagecoach. The piebald horse had been harnessed wrong, now at the wheel side of the coach, I noticed. Andy glanced at me and grinned as we reached the stage, proud of his cleverness. One of the farmers stood holding the reins to their saddle ponies.

Farmers? I don't know why I continued to think of them as that. Now they were nothing but thieves and killers. They had found an easier way to make a living than scratching it out of the reluctant earth. None of them would ever return to a laboring life no matter what they might have convinced themselves.

'Where are you taking us?' Marly asked.

'Not far,' Andy answered as the two farmers loaded the strongbox into the coach's boot.

'Then why . . . ?'

'You can't ride with one of those on your pony's back,' Andy said, nodding at the heavy strongbox containing the gold shipment. 'We're going to haul it off the way it was hauled in.'

'You can't get away with it, Andy,' I said.

'Sure I can. We have so far, haven't we? We're just going to use the coach to haul the box away. Off the stage route. Someplace hidden. Then we're going to crack it, divvy up the gold and ride our separate ways.' He shrugged. 'It's not difficult, Keogh, if you take a while to figure things out.'

One of the farmers had clambered on to the stagecoach box and gathered the reins. 'We'd better quit yakking and get moving,' he said. 'That fire might bring somebody.'

'You're right,' Andy agreed, calling for his appaloosa to be brought up. 'Mosely, you want to help the ladies aboard?'

'I'm not going,' Marly said, resisting the hand one of the farmers had placed on her shoulder. Her eyes met mine with stubborn fear.

'Sure you are,' Andy said. He took her roughly by her other shoulder and the two men forced her up into the coach to sit beside Eva who seemed to have lost the power of resistance. She sat staring at the floor of the coach as Bull Mosely swung heavily aboard.

Fury was building in me. I turned Andy roughly toward me. 'You said that nothing would happen to Marly!'

'Did I? I don't recall saying that,' Andy answered, the smile gone from his face. 'Don't worry, Keogh. I've kind of lost interest in the girl. She's just going along for the ride as a hostage. You just remember that I have her, and if you get any ideas about following me — well, then something just *might* happen to her.'

'Follow along?' I said numbly. 'I'm not going with you?'

'You!' Andy laughed harshly. 'Keogh, what would I need you along for?'

I started to make an angry move, but knew it was futile. Four armed men were watching me. Andy swung into the appaloosa's saddle and shouted for the party to move.

There was absolutely nothing I could do but stand and watch as the stage-coach rolled away, Marly's pleading eyes watching me until they were out of sight. I started trudging back toward the stage stop, cursing all the way.

Blair and the stage crew stood watching me from the front of the adobe where they had rushed to recover their guns before realizing that there was no one to use them against. Behind them smoke still billowed into the clear morning sky. Through the open door of the building I could see the last of the roof beams, blackened and broken, the few pockets of still-burning flame licking at the walls of the destroyed way-station.

'What are you doing back here?' Blair demanded. His sallow face was now soot-darkened. There was a hangdog look about him. To one side, Allie and the shotgun rider stood glowering at me. The birdlike little woman, Jane, sat on a round rock nearby, her face buried in her hands. Mrs. Revere stood beside her, murmuring words we could not hear. No one had yet removed Jane's husband's body from the doorway.

'Where else would you have me go? Look, Blair — I wasn't with them. If I was, I'd be gone.' I spotted my pistol just outside the door where I had dropped it and stepped up on to the porch to retrieve it. No one tried to stop me. I thought unhappily that it was going to do me as much good as their weapons were. I asked:

'Aren't there any other horses around here?'

'They've been scattered. You saw the corral.'

'Well, what are you going to do then?' I wanted to know.

'Wait for the next stage to come through. It should get here around noon,' Allie answered.

'What about the bandits? The kidnapped women?' I asked the red-bearded man. He shook his head and replied:

'Mister, the company pays me to drive their stagecoaches, not to track down highway robbers.'

'Something has to be done,' I said frantically, thinking of Marly and Eva. 'What about you, Blair!'

'What would you have me do?' Blair asked. 'Walk after them?'

He was right, of course. There was nothing that could be done. I stared dismally into the distance. I had tried to help the women, but that was of no consolation to them now. Andy Givens, damn him, had outsmarted me.

Desperation brought a grim sort of determination with it. Looking southward, the direction Andy had ridden, I said to Blair, 'Why not? Why not try to walk after them?' The man looked at me as if I had gone mad. Maybe I had. 'Look,' I said, 'they won't want to travel far with the stagecoach. Spotted anywhere off the coach trail it's a dead give-away that something's wrong. They'll have to stop, break into the strongbox and divide up the gold, won't they? There's a chance — '

'You're crazy!' Blair muttered. Then he turned glumly away. Warren Travers had eased up beside me, looking haunted.

'Do you think you can do it?' the mine owner asked.

'Who knows? It seems unlikely, but I can't just stand here.'

'If you could recover the gold . . . '

'That is completely unlikely,' I said.

The mine boss's eyes were pouched, weary.

'The gold was mine, Keogh,' he told me. He lifted his hand as if he were going to grip my shirt, but it fell away again.

'I know it. Everyone knows it. There was practically no one you didn't tell that the stage was carrying gold. Why do you think the bandits decided to hit us? You talk too much, Travers.'

'I know I do,' he said miserably. 'I thought the shipment was safe enough. I even hired a line detective, him,' he said nodding at Blair, 'to help safeguard the shipment. A lot of good that did me. But the gold . . . I need it badly, Keogh. I lost a fortune when I had a shaft cave-in at my Number Two mine. I have to dig it out, start over. The gold was to start over, to repay debts owed. I'm ruined if I can't recover it.'

'It looks like you're ruined, then, Travers,' was all I could say. I turned my back then and started away. Now he did grab my arm. I shook his hand off.

'You're going ahead anyway?' he asked in puzzlement.

'I have to. There's something that the bandits have that's more valuable than all your gold. I'm going after them.'

'There's a reward, even for a partial recovery — ' he pled to my back. I kept walking away, striding through the oaks where I hoped to find the wagon tracks and somehow follow the stolen stage-coach. Futile as it seemed, still I had to try. Succeed or fail. Marly would expect it of me.

The tracks weren't hard to find, and I walked on, trying not to think about the distances ahead of me, the raw land and bitter wind which was beginning to rise to chill me to the bones. I tried not to think about my battered hands and the small protection my wrong-side-slung pistol would provide against four armed men.

Perhaps Andy would keep his word this time, I thought hopefully. Maybe he would release Marly. Eva, however, was a different proposition. She had been a part of the bargaining price when he fell in with Bull Mosely. Bull would not let her go. That meant that Marly would never again be the woman that she was. She had devoted her life, rightly or wrongly, to her sister.

Andy Givens. What would he do? In the past few days he had murdered two men, showed signs of madness so that I scarcely recognized him. Would he actually be willing to split the gold with Bull Mosely and the other bandits?

I had no answers to any of my questions, but they spun constantly through my mind as I trudged along over the broken ground, my ribs aching, my feet, tight in my Western boots, unsuitable for hiking, already beginning to blister.

The sun rose higher and the land to grow even rougher. Ahead I saw only rocky crags, tangled red canyons, stacks of gray boulders. No stage-coach could make it across that section of land, not unless the bandits knew of a hidden trail — and none of them was familiar with this part of Colorado. At least I did not think so. That broken land would be where they intended to hide the coach, break open the strongbox and split the gold, make plans. I knew that. It had to be. I tried to hurry on, but even with a renewed sense of urgency my body could do no more.

Was I too late? They could have finished their task and ridden on their way already. Even if I did find them, then what? Rush the camp with my pistol only to be shot down? It was a desperate man who now climbed a rock-strewn knoll, skirted a broad patch of nopal cactus and slid, stumbled, half fell down the far side of the rise.

I had to stop. Not for the sake of my battered body, but because it was senseless to charge on farther into these broken hills without an idea of where I was going. I halted, my breathing ragged, looking and listening for any small sign of life: a bit of color, a low voice, the whicker of a horse.

Or — angry shouts, women scream-
ing, gunshots blaring out, echoing
down the long canyons.

8

The day continued silent, cold, the twist of canyons below me empty and forbidding. The wind sang among the tangled rocks, mocking me. I could not go aimlessly on, but neither could I stand and wait as time ran past. Who knew what notion the bandits might take now that they were alone with Eva and Marly, hidden from the world? Bull Mosely would protect Eva, saving her for himself, but who was there to protect Marly? I started on again, staggering down the rough hillside, small stones rolling beneath my boots. Twice I fell, crashing to the stony ground. Twice I rose. A few more bruises and scrapes were of no importance anymore. I only hoped I wouldn't be careless enough to misstep and twist an ankle, break a leg.

I reached the floor of a narrow

canyon with high-rising red bluffs shadowing it, blocking out sun and sky. I held my broken ribs, they would not be ignored, tried to force the chill air into my lungs. I was a fool even to attempt this trek. I was lost myself now, and hadn't the strength to climb out of the canyon and reach the stage station again even had I wished. I rubbed an elbow I had torn open in one of my falls and looked skyward. Two hours had passed, at a guess, since the stage had been taken. A lot could happen in two hours. I looked down for easier footing.

And saw them. Twin ruts carved into the red sand of the canyon floor where a wheeled vehicle had passed.

It had to be the stagecoach. What other wagon could possibly have come this way? There were no ranches, no farms, no towns around here, and if there were, certainly they would have an easier trail to use than this uneven, sand-and-rock wash. My heart rate lifted and I felt a surge of eagerness.

Still I hesitated.

The questions remained. Was I just to walk up to them — assuming they had not already abandoned the coach and ridden off on their separate ways? Four Winchesters against my badly-slung Colt. They would shoot me down before I had even gotten in pistol range.

My purpose, however, also remained the same. I had to find Marly and get her away from this murdering crew. I started on blindly, without a plan, with only desperate hope.

I came around a bend in the ravine and was suddenly in sight of the stagecoach. There was no one on or near it, and my heart sank. The robbers had taken care of their business already and departed. My silent curse was vicious and bitter.

I started on. The horses were still hitched to the coach. The piebald saw me approaching and stamped a hoof, rolling its eye at me nastily as if I were another human come to make his life still more miserable. I peered cautiously into the coach compartment. No one. Nothing. I had begun to step forward when I heard a voice ahead of me. I froze in my tracks and crouched low, snaking my Colt from my holster.

They were arguing. Crouched around the broken-open gold chest like vultures. I heard Andy clearly saying, 'That's the split, if you don't like it . . .' Then his words faded away in the wind. Remaining in a crouch, I narrowed my eyes and searched for and found — the women.

Marly and Eva sat together on a rocky bench overlooking the wash. Eva had her head resting on Marly's shoulder. She must have been feeling over-whelmed, lost again after a few brief hours of hope. Mosely had bartered for her and she had been stolen away. Her future must have seemed too bleak to imagine. Marly's head came up and I imagined that she could see me across the distance between us, even though common sense told me that she could not.

Now was the time. It was the only chance I was likely to get. The four men huddled around the gold. Bickering over the amount of their shares, it seemed. I could have told them that it was of no use. I could have cautioned them against arguing with Andy Givens about anything. Right now my mind was busy with other matters, trying to devise a plan. I knew roughly what I intended to do, but there was no way of predicting the outcome. Is there ever, in any enterprise?

Easing my way forward, my eyes on the bandits whose attention was diverted now, I stretched up one hand and exerting all of the pressure I could, managed to slip the stagecoach's brake. Still no one had glanced my way. They were intent on dividing their fortune. I stepped away a little, keeping the coach between the outlaws and myself. Crouching, I scoured the ground for a few rough, fist-sized rocks.

With a silent apology to the dumb animal I took aim and flung one of these at the flank of the piebald horse. He tossed his head angrily and whickered in annoyance. My second stone took him nearly on the same spot, and he bolted ahead, the team following him out of necessity.

I heard one of the bandits yell, saw eyes widen and men come to their feet and try to dive aside. It was already too late. The stampeded horses had no room to turn aside in the close confines of the canyon, and towing the stagecoach behind them, they raced through the bandits, the terrifying thunder of their hoofs loud and ominous.

I saw one man go down beneath the hoofs of the horses, another trip as he tried to make his escape and be similarly trampled. As he tried to rise again, the heavy wheels of the stagecoach rolled over him and he stayed down for good.

I withdrew behind a stony outcropping the size of a door and pressed myself against the walls of the cliff, my Colt clenched tightly in my left hand, hammer eared back. I could see nothing through the dust cloud, but I did see Marly and Eva, high enough up the rocks to be out of harm's way, stand and stare in awe. Eva had her hands to her mouth; Marly was trying to look down the canyon, perhaps to try to determine if more help might be arriving or if the runaway stage had simply been an accident. I eased out a little from my rocky shelter, trying to get a better look. And found I had shown myself.

One of the bandits shouted, lifted a pointing finger in my direction and raised his Winchester to his shoulder. A .44-40 slug spanged off the rock face, showering me with stone fragments. I took a shot back with my pistol, but must have missed entirely. My left-handed work was just no good. Andy had been right — I couldn't hit a kitchen wall if I were locked inside the room.

I fired again, but the bandit didn't even flinch as I shot.

He just folded up, dead, his face grinding into the red-sand floor of the canyon. I had gotten him with a chance shot! Or so I thought. Then I saw Andy Givens standing a few yards behind the bandit, his Colt curling smoke.

Andy had shot his own man down!

I knew he hadn't done it to save my hide. Although Andy could not see me, he must have felt certain who it was that was crazy enough to trail them out there on foot. He knew it was me, no doubt, but Andy hadn't been trying to save my life; I was sure of that. He had simply taken the chance to divide the gold in a way more to his liking.

'Keogh!' he yelled, and I was dumb enough to peer around the shoulder of the rock. Andy Givens fired three rounds through the barrel of his pistol, and any one of them could have killed me if I had been inches farther out of my shelter. 'Just remember that, Keogh. Back off.'

He had known that his bullets couldn't tag me in my hiding place. He had done it to keep me back, but more, Andy Givens had been showing off! In the middle of the carnage, panicked horses, dying men beside him, Andy Givens had taken the time to show off for me, perhaps for the women, once again.

I knew what I was facing with Andy. He was a dead shot. I wouldn't doubt that he could shoot my ears off had I shown myself. I didn't know who else — how many — I was facing. I didn't know what would be done now with the women. I had to take another look, no matter that the lead was flying. The day grew cooler; the sun nearly completely blocked by the thrusting walls of the canyon, but I was sweating. Perspiration ran down my spine and trickled into my eyes. Yet I had to have another look to see what was happening.

I went to my belly where I figured to be less of a target and inched my way forward a few inches. The dust was settling and I could see more clearly now. One man had been trampled to death. He lay unmoving against the canyon floor, his body broken. The rifleman Andy had shot lay nearby, his Winchester still in his hand. That left Andy and Mosely unaccounted for.

One of them had caught up the stagecoach team as the horses, stymied in their effort to escape from the wedge of the canyon, had given it up. Now Andy — or Mosely — backed the team until they and the stage provided cover for where they had been dividing the gold. I could see neither man.

Nor could I see Marly and Eva any longer!

In frustration I shouted at Andy, my voice unnaturally high. 'Andy, let the women go! There's a dozen men not far behind me. You'll never outrun them taking the women along.'

No one answered. Probably because no one believed me. I could almost picture Andy Givens smiling to himself, shaking his head at my foolishness.

I stood watching, waiting. For a moment there was a flurry of activity and then what I thought was the creak of saddle leather. Then silence. I waited in my hiding place until I could take it no longer, then slowly I crept out, my hand cramped around my pistol grips, my legs knotted with the day's walking, my ribs continuing to burn. I eased my way forward, keeping as near the cliff face as possible. Inch by inch I made my way, ready to exchange lead at any moment. I needn't have been so cautious in my movements.

They were gone.

Andy, Mosely and the women had vanished up the canyon, leaving me behind with the two dead men. I stooped and snatched up the fallen man's Winchester, feeling more comfortable with that than with my left-handed gun. Then I started away, after them. After only a few steps I halted and turned back toward the stagecoach. I dropped the trace chains to the team and freed them to make their way home in harness, leaving the coach behind.

But not before I had unsheathed my bowie and cut the piebald from his harness. The tall horse continued to give me the evil eye as if he suspected that I was responsible for the stones hitting his rump. Still, he was fairly patient with me, perhaps because the only men he knew who unharnessed him were those who meant to take him to the stable, rub him down and feed him.

When he discovered my true intentions, I did not know what the result might be. Returning to the stage, I cut a ten-foot length of leather from the reins and began fashioning the crudest sort of hackamore. I meant to ride that horse. I doubted he had ever been broken to saddle, but I had broken more than a few broncs in my time. None of them had been delighted with the prospect. This big dray horse would be completely different, but I doubted he was any tougher than those little mustangs that Andy and I used to bust for ten dollars a head. I settled a loop

156

over the piebald's head. That was easy. He was used to standing in place to be harnessed as well. The problem would come when I tried to clamber on to his back and stay there without a saddle.

I turned the team, swatted the lead bay on his rump and set them running. The piebald naturally wanted to run with them, but I held him back. Again that was easier than I had expected it to be, and it was a good thing. The shape my hands were in, I could never have held him if he put all of his effort and muscle into running.

I began talking to the horse. 'You aren't going to like this, but we are going to do it. We don't have much time to teach you the rules, but we have no choice. I can't run them down afoot again.'

I slipped the hackamore over his muzzle, and he stood for that as well. Maybe, I thought with shallow optimism, the horse had even been ridden before. Maybe some stable kid used to take him for rides. Maybe.

I stroked the big horse's muzzle, ran my hand along his quivering flank and mounted him quick — Indian-style. I was on his back before he knew it.

I was off again before *I* knew it.

Bunching his muscles, he had arched his back and tossed me neatly. I landed on my shoulder and skull. I rose again wearily. At the second attempt he let me stay mounted. Maybe I had just surprised him the first time with my sudden mount. No matter the reason, I was grateful for his change in attitude. Now what? I was going to try to catch up with four well-trained saddle ponies on this lumbering coach-horse who had no idea what it was that I wanted him to do. My only positive thought was that those ponies, burdened down as they were with the stolen gold, would need to be rested somewhere, sometime before the sun set. If I could get the piebald moving in the right direction there was a chance.

The piebald would mind the hackamore, I thought, being used to reins. If only I could once get him started. I heeled him a couple of times, but he didn't get the idea. His lifelong signal to move was a snap of a bullwhip. I tried a crude substitute. Yelling 'Haw-yup' as I had heard Allie shout to start his team, I flicked the piebald's ear with the finish end of the reins.

And we started forward up the canyon, the piebald seeming confused, but determined.

It was anything but an easy horse to ride, but I was riding the big rebel. I was hoping that over the miles his intelligence would cause him to come to understand what was required of him. Only time would tell. In the meantime, I clung to the piebald, following the tracks the other horses had imprinted in the sandy earth.

I glanced skyward. I needed to find the route Andy and Mosely had taken out of the canyon before full dark, or all would be lost. Even then, I thought unhappily, my chances of following were not good. They had a lead on me, good ponies under them, and a destination in mind.

The sky was purple with twilight before I found the foot of the trail leading up and out of the canyon. It was a surprisingly easy trail to follow, formed apparently by rains washing down loose soil from the heights. Cresting out of the canyon I halted the piebald, after a few false tries, and sat staring across the wild land where Marly had vanished. The western horizon was deep purple, burnt orange with a few high scarlet pennants where clouds lingered. It would grow rapidly dark now, and much colder before long.

I looked for any signs of habitation, for any road scratched into the long country. I saw nothing at all promising. I simply took my bearings by studying the direction the tracks were tending and orienting myself by the evening star which had appeared low on the horizon with the sunset.

I assumed that Andy would now beeline it toward his destination. There was no need for deviousness, for laying false trails or changing direction.

What did he have to fear? One battered cowboy without a prayer of catching up with them? I heeled the piebald, and this time he understood, moving forward at his heavy pace down the grassy knolls ahead of us, into the steadily darkening night.

The hours staggered past. I was used to sitting a horse — that was how I made my living — but riding this broad-backed dray animal without a saddle as it plodded on at its ungainly pace was beyond wearying. It was not all the piebald's fault, of course. My legs, using a different set of muscles, ached from my long trek after the bandits. My right hand was useless for controlling the makeshift reins of the hackamore, my left little better. My head ached, my ribs were hot with pain. I'm not sure, had I fallen from the piebald's back at that moment, that I would have had the strength to remount.

And so I clung to the big animal and continued blindly through the night.

It must have been close to ten o'clock when I saw — thought I saw — distant lights. They were so distant and feeble that it was difficult to be sure. No brighter than fireflies, they blinked across the wide range. The palest star in the sky was no brighter. Still, I eased the piebald's head in that direction and we plodded on.

Within half an hour I was sure. They were man-made lights. Some sort of tiny hamlet or settlement, a ranch house, perhaps. Would Andy have ridden toward it? He needed fresh horses; the amount of gold he was carrying would have worn his mounts down, even his big appaloosa. They likely would have had no food with them, either. I had no way of knowing — perhaps Andy had decided to steer clear of any community as he struck out toward the south, wary of local law. I had no choice but to go with my instincts or ride aimlessly over the dark plains. We continued toward the lights which grew larger and brighter by the mile.

To my surprise we suddenly cut a traveled road. There were wagon ruts here and the sign of many horses passing. Would the outlaw Andy Givens instinctively avoid the road, or being as bold as he was, follow it carelessly? I knew Andy as well as any man, but nevertheless, not well enough to out-guess him — that had already been proven. I thought that with weary ponies and two exhausted women accompanying him, he would have opted for the level road rather than risking breaking a horse's leg in the rough country surrounding. I turned the piebald on to the road that led to the distant town.

Steadily the horse clomped on. I felt like some Quixote on an aimless, frustrated search. What did I really think I could do against Andy and Mosely? I shook off the doubts once again. They were of no help to Marly and her sister.

I came abreast of the camp suddenly, without recognizing it for what it was. Fifty feet, no more, off the road I saw the dark unmistakable silhouettes of two horses, a campfire that would have fit inside a bowler hat, a thin tendril of smoke twisting its way skyward. I let my horse walk on past it, and halted a hundred yards up the road. There could be dozens of reasons someone would camp there. But anyone approaching the town would surely have ridden that last mile. Anyone with a reason to be traveling away from it would surely have put more miles under his pony's hoofs before halting for night camp.

Unless a man was trying to remain unseen. Hiding out.

In the darkness I slipped from the big black-and-white horse's back, my borrowed Winchester in my hand, and began circling back toward the hidden camp. There were stands of sumac here, and purple sage, and it was easy enough to conceal myself by moving in a crouch. It was not so easy to move stealthily, letting no sound escape as my boots shuffled over the broken quartz soil underfoot. I crept forward, rifle in hand, hoping that the piebald would not, having smelled the other horses, whicker to them. I put my foot down on a barrel cactus and winced as a needle-sharp spine drove through my boot. I paused, stilled my breath and eased my way forward, toward the tiny camp, using the scent of woodsmoke as my compass.

The night was too starbright for my liking; fortunately, we had a late-rising moon just then, and it was dark enough yet for me to be only a shadow among the shadows.

I nearly blundered into the camp before I had seen it beyond the screen of brush. I pulled back, heart racing, both hands on the Winchester. I heard one voice and then the other. Again I crept forward in an uneasy crouch.

And saw Bull Mosely, blanket across his big shoulders, talking to Eva Pierce.

9

Bull had a small tin cup of coffee in his big hand. Eva, her shoulders also covered by a blanket, sat huddled near the fire, her eyes turned down, her head hanging. One of the horses across the camp was suddenly alerted by my presence and it lifted its head, backing uneasily away from the unidentified intruder. For all it knew I was a prowling predator. And, it seemed, that was exactly what I was.

I was angry, a fierce determination rising in me. Bull Mosely spoke again, and although I could not hear his words clearly, I did not like them. He was bulking large over Eva, hovering in a menacing attitude. He tossed his coffee away and lifted her chin with his thumb. You cannot hear a silent cry for help, but I seemed to at that moment.

I did not see Andy, nor Marly, did

not know if Andy's guns were waiting for me in the dark of night, but there is a time for rashness, and as Bull bent lower over Eva, I decided that the time had come. I stepped into the clearing.

'Back off or die, Bull!' I said too loudly.

The big man rose, spun recognized me by the flickering firelight.

'You! Andy warned me — '

At the same time his right hand dipped into his holster and came up with his revolver. There was an angry glitter in his eye, a frustrated look on his face. He had been so near to his goal.

I lifted the Winchester to my shoulder and shot him with no more compunction than I would have had for a cougar preying on a new-born calf. Mosely's eyes went blank. The pistol dropped from his outflung hand and he staggered away, falling on his back against the tiny campfire, extinguishing it. He did not move again.

I walked into the camp circle

cautiously, still not knowing where Andy Givens might be. Eva had drawn herself up even tighter, into a pathetic, blanket-covered ball. I could see her shaking beneath it.

'It's me, Eva,' I said as gently as I could. I started to bend, to touch her, but I did not think she wanted that sort of physical reassurance just then. 'It's Corey Keogh, Eva,' I told her. 'Get up, pull yourself together. We're not out of this yet.'

'Is he — ?' she murmured.

'Quite,' I assured her. 'He'll never bother you again. For now,' I said more roughly, 'get up. I need your help.'

'What do you want me to do, Corey?' she asked, opening her hands and looking at me for the first time. I crouched down beside her.

'In a minute. Eva, I have to know — where is Marly? Where did Andy take her?'

'Into the town. Andy wanted to buy fresh horses.' Eva's voice was muffled and uncertain.

'Why didn't you all go together?' I asked her.

'Andy told Mosely that with both of us there — Marly and me — we might decide to try asking the townspeople for help. With me being held out here, Marly would never jeopardize my well-being.'

'I see. All right, then, Mosely was left here to watch you — which must have suited him fine.'

'It did, he, Mosely, was to guard me and the rest of the gold. Andy could hardly have gone into a stable with thousands of dollars in stolen gold in his saddlebags. Even unloading them from his appaloosa's back would have been a give-away.'

'You mean that the gold is here!'

'It's under those rocks across the camp,' she said, lifting her chin in that direction. 'Take it; no one cares.'

'I don't either, Eva. I only care about Marly, can't you understand?'

'You know I didn't — ' Her words were still broken as she shivered beneath her blanket. 'I didn't really know that it was like that between you two. I guess I have been so concerned with my own wants and needs — '

'That doesn't matter, Eva. Tell it all to Marly when you see her again.'

'If I see her again,' she said weakly.

'You will,' I promised with a confidence I did not feel. 'For now, get up and do what I tell you. I still need your help.'

'All right,' Eva said with a resoluteness I had never heard in her voice before. Perhaps all that had gone before was strengthening her. Or maybe she had at last come to realize how much of a burden she had been laying on her younger sister while she dithered, sighed and felt sorry for herself. Eva got unsteadily to her feet, keeping her eyes turned away from the dead man sprawled across the still-smoking fire.

'What do you want me to do?' Eva asked.

'I need you to saddle those two ponies, yours and Mosely's. I still can't handle the job with my right hand broken up like it is. Can you manage?'

'If needs be,' she said, with a sort of frail determination.

'Good. I need a manageable horse to ride. And you,' I said without joy, 'need a mount to carry you away from here.'

'I have to go with you!' Eva said, astonished.

'No. You can't, Eva. That's that. If you are safely away, I will have a better chance of it with Marly. Andy won't be able to hold the threat of harming you over her head as he has been.'

'But, Corey — ' Eva looked around her at the cold, star-shadowed endless plains, 'I don't know where to ride. I have no idea how to do it on my own!'

'Eva,' I told her, partly to convince her, partly to convince myself. 'You are a stronger woman than you have been *willing* to be up until now. I know this. Marly has told me something about your past. It has made you willing to be weak. Well, now is the time to shed that. Copperfield may find you some day and again bundle you in security. But for now, for tonight, be the woman you can be.

'Strike out toward the North Star and keep riding until you can find someone to help you. Marly needs me now more than you do.'

She was clumsy and inefficient at it, but she managed to get the two ponies saddled. Swinging awkwardly into the saddle on Mosely's sturdy dun pony I felt more at home than I had for a long while. The horse was weary, but we would not be riding far.

Eva, meanwhile, had gotten into leather aboard the bay horse she had been riding, her skirts spread. I could almost see her blush in the night — she was unused to riding astraddle. I repeated the instructions I had given her. They were the best I could do: walk the pony toward the Polar Star and hope for dawn. I also gave her Bull Mosely's handgun. She did not like having the dead man's pistol, but it did give her some sense of security. As she turned the horse to depart, I briefly held its bridle and promised her:

'I'll bring Marly to you soon. Denver if not before there. Trust me, Eva.'

'Corey — I am beginning to trust you more than any man I have ever known.'

Then she heeled the horse and was gone into the night, vanished across the land. Her words echoed in my mind, and I wondered what had caused her to speak them. Wondered if I could live up to such praise.

I started the dun pony toward the distant town.

I did not find the piebald along the road, and figured that he had gotten tired of my company and decided to choose his own way. I couldn't blame him a lot. I didn't worry about the big horse. He would manage to toss that hackamore in no time and either find some less demanding human companions or return to free graze.

The dun was sluggish, but well-mannered. As we drew nearer to the town, however, he became high-stepping, anxious. Ahead of him now were those man-places where new hay and oats, fresh water were held in abundance. He sensed this and I had to draw in the reins just a little to control his eagerness.

If the town had a name, I never learned what it was.

Sleepy, wind-swept, forlorn, it was about half the size of Tulip. More shabby, weather-beaten wooden buildings, a line of low adobes, a single elm tree which must have been the civic pride standing alone in a deserted plaza in the center of town. I wasn't there to criticize or sightsee. I needed to begin by finding the local stables. Andy would have seen to the business of obtaining fresh horses first.

There might have been several scattered around town, but I did what any stranger would have done and halted at the first I happened to see. I swung down heavily from my horse and entered the dank interior of the barnlike structure. There was no one around. I let my eyes run over the horses that stood watching me curiously from over the gates to their stalls.

And there stood Andy's appaloosa. The animal seemed to recognize me, and I strode that way to stroke his neck, noting that he was badly gaunted after his long run.

'Help you?' an unfriendly voice from behind me asked, and I turned to see a round ball of a man with a red face watching me.

'The appy belongs to a friend of mine. I was looking for him — we got separated on the trail.'

'Is that so?' the round man asked me with skepticism. Considering the way I looked, maybe he took me for a runaway outlaw — which I was — or a horse thief.

I took a few steps toward him, trying to force a smile. 'True, friend. You happen to know where he went? Curly-headed, sort of cocky gent.'

'My only business is horses,' the stableman told me. 'Now, is there anything I can do for you in that line.'

I considered. 'Maybe. I have no cash money, but I've a dun pony out front with a lot of leg and a deep chest. Trouble is, he's weary and I have to keep travelling. If you'd consider a straight-across swap for a fresh horse, I'd be willing.'

All of that seemed only to deepen the man's suspicions, to cause him to be more certain that I was a man on the run, otherwise what was my hurry? The light of profit was in his eyes, however, and he said: 'Let me take a look at him.'

He examined Mosely's dun, giving out a little grunt now and then as he felt its legs for heat, bent his head to listen to its chest. Straightening, he said, 'We can talk if you are willing to kick in twenty dollars or so.'

'Haven't got it,' I said.

He shook his head, scratched it and muttered to himself. Still he was interested, I could see. I knew I would get the worst of any bargain he offered — experience had taught me that

— but a fresh pony might make the difference, Andy now being mounted on a well-rested animal himself. 'If you don't much care about bloodlines or looks,' the round man said with practiced hesitancy, 'I got a chuckle-headed, dumpy little sorrel some broke-down cowboy left here a few weeks ago. I'm tired of feeding the damn thing, to tell you the truth, and I'll never sell it. I'll trade you straight across for the dun.'

'If it's fresh, I'll take it,' I answered, and I was shown the sorriest-looking, stumpy sorrel I had ever seen. Shaggy and wall-eyed it looked at me lethargically as we entered the stall. No wonder its last owner had abandoned it. Nevertheless, I shifted my saddle to the sorry little horse and left the stable, considering that after all I had lost nothing, the dun having belonged to Bull Mosely.

The stableman, after getting the better of me in the swap, and knowing it, had loosened up enough to give me a description of the horses he had sold to Andy Givens: a blue roan with a white tail, a chestnut with a blaze. On my dumpy sorrel, I began to scour the town for them.

Where, I asked myself, would Andy be? Not at a hotel — he wouldn't wish to sleep a night away with Mosely guarding all that gold. The nearest general store, for provisions, then maybe a hasty meal at a restaurant if he was sure enough of Marly that he felt confident she would not try to break away and run?

Which she would not, believing that Bull Mosely still held Eva captive.

I passed two restaurants, both shuttered — it was only a few hours before dawn — and one general store, also closed down. I frowned. It had been after midnight when Andy had decided to come into the town to exchange horses; had he just shifted saddles and hit the return trail, pausing for nothing else?

No, I decided. No matter what, if

Andy was to make a run for it, he would have to have some sort of provisions with him. A man doesn't run far or fast on an empty stomach. I sat the woolly little sorrel and pondered, trying to put myself in Andy Givens's frame of mind. It was so simple an explanation that I wondered at my own stupidity, not for the first time.

Whatever Andy wanted, he took. He cared nothing for locks. If the general stores were closed, he would simply find a back door and break into it. I guided the placid sorrel through an alley and emerged behind the town's main street where all was dark. A grove of cottonwoods cast star-shadows across the littered back yards of the businesses there. I could make out the hint of the rising sun, only a pale arc of light above the eastern horizon, like beaten copper.

Behind the general store I saw two horses standing patiently in the shadows.

A tall blue roan with a white tail and a leggy chestnut with a white blaze on its nose.

10

The back door to the store stood open, and I saw hurried, shadowy movement within. I silently levered a round into the breech of my Winchester, swung carefully down from the sorrel and started that way through the night shadows. I had the element of surprise on my side, and I thought, stealth to aid me, but Andy Givens had the eyes of a cat, and instincts to match. Before I had gotten within thirty feet of the back door, Andy leaped from the interior of the building, went into a crouch and fanned three rapid shots through his Colt's barrel.

The light was bad, otherwise I knew that Andy would have had me. He does not miss. I dropped to one knee and fired a single shot from my Winchester. I saw Andy stagger and twist away. The sack of provisions he had been carrying was left abandoned as he dashed toward the blue roan, throwing two more wild shots across his body at me, causing me to dive to the ground.

He turned his big horse's head, and the roan reared up, making another clean shot impossible. One last pistol report from Andy's Colt let me know that he still had teeth. Then he was gone, spurring the blue roan through the stand of Cottonwood trees, racing toward open country. Across town, lanterns were lit and a few people wandered forward to see what had happened.

Marly stood in the doorway, small and bewildered, and I walked to her.

I did not plan it, but I took her in my arms and kissed the top of her head. I could feel her shivering in my arms, and when she looked up at me her cheeks were damp with tears.

'I knew you would come, Corey. I just kept telling myself that you would come for me.'

I had to force myself to release her,

but I did. With a sternness I did not feel, I said: 'Marly, you must stay here. Do not leave town, no matter what.'

'What are you going to do?' she asked, her eyes searching mine in the poor dawn light.

'I'm going after Andy. He's gone bad, Marly. He'll do this again and again to other people if I don't stop him now.'

'I have to go with you!' Marly said, clutching at my shirt front. 'Eva is — '

'Eva is all right,' I said as calmly as I could. 'Believe me. I sent her away, back toward the Denver stage line. She should be just about there by now. She will be fine, Marly. You,' I repeated roughly, 'you stay here! It will be all right.'

Would it? I did not know as I pulled away from her and returned to my sorrel. Swinging into the saddle I saw her watching me, forlorn and confused. I forced my eyes away and turned the sorrel eastward. What I had told Marly was true — I had to finish off Andy Givens. He would kill and kill again, given the chance, and here, now, I was the only man who could stop him before he did.

I rode steadily toward the rising sun, without a hope of keeping up with Andy on his fresh, leggy blue roan, but confident that I knew where to find him, certain that he would still be there when I arrived, searching wildly for the gold which I had taken a minute to move to a new place of concealment.

Frustrated in his quest, what would Andy do? I knew him too well. He would know what had happened, and figured who had done it to him. I was the only one foolish enough to continue this mad pursuit. He would know who had done it, would know that I was following still. And he would lay a trap to kill me.

First, of course, he would have to extract the gold's location from me, by any means necessary. He no longer had the women captive to use as leverage, and so he would have to resort to torture of some kind, although the thought made me smile grimly. My body had been so broken and battered over the last few days that I wondered if I hadn't grown immune to pain. But no man is.

I tried to put myself in Andy's place again. Returning to the camp he finds Mosely dead, Eva gone. *Keogh*, he thinks instantly, as he searches desperately for the stolen gold. Then, realizing that I have not yet done with him, he needs to come up with a scheme for ambushing me while taking me alive so that I can reveal the location of the gold.

That was as far as my reckoning went. Andy was devious enough to come up with any number of plans. I could only wait and see and be ready — to gun him down at first sight. Like the rabid lobo wolf he was.

The sun was brightening, piercing through my eyes into my brain. I needed sleep, rest, food. Marly was waiting for me. Why not just let Andy go, forget this mad pursuit? I was crazy.

I had been told that before, and now I was beginning to believe it. I was no lawman, no angel of retribution, only a half-smart cowboy, broken and battered.

I rode on, the sorrel eager enough, but nothing but a stumblebum in his movements. Like me.

The glare of the morning sun was far too bright to look into now. I was nearly to the camp and would need my vision. Since I did not dare approach the clearing on horseback anyway, I halted the sorrel and swung down, stiff in every muscle of my body. I had to pause for a moment, leaning against the horse until a spell of dizziness passed. Then, rifle in hand, I began to circle the camp, moving through the sumac and sage as I had when I had caught up with Mosely there.

The insects had come awake with the sun and a cloud of gnats swanned around my face and remained there as I eased through the tangle of chaparral, trying to make no sound at all, trying not to breathe loudly. Andy was there, somewhere, he with the eyes of a cat and the ears of a wolf.

I inched along the trail, still unable to see the camp. The laurel-leaf sumac had a fresh, pungent scent to it, the sage was heavy in the air. I stepped aside a low-growing barrel cactus, with a painful remembrance of my last encounter with one. The sky had begun to pale, only a single line of beaten gold limning the eastern horizon and the birds had taken to morning wing. Doves by the hundreds going to water passed overhead, cutting sharp silhouettes. A cottontail rabbit, startled by my appearance, bounded away after a moment's incredulous glance.

I saw the camp through the screen of surrounding brush, and eased nearer, moving in a crouch.

Mosely's body had been moved from the fire ring. Andy must have searched beneath the body for the saddlebags containing the gold. Fortunately, I had not been clever enough to consider such a hiding place.

Where was Andy!

I saw his blue roan, head down, grazing. The dead body of Mosely continued to stare unblinkingly at the pale crystal of the sky. A butcher bird flitted past, seeking insect prey. Not far away a mule deer eyed me and slipped silently back into the brush. I waited. My neck began to itch. My hands were cramped around the rifle I carried. He had to be here, somewhere. He had to make some move, some sound. Andy was too rash to play a waiting game forever. I held my crouch, wiping at my eyes which now began to sting with perspiration. I shifted my position only by inches and heard the muffled, unmistakable ratcheting of a Colt revolver's hammer being drawn back. I froze.

'Where is it, Keogh?' Andy said.

'I don't get you, Andy.'

'I want the gold, Keogh,' Andy said. I heard him step nearer, I felt the muzzle of his revolver nudge my back between my shoulder blades. His voice was almost carefree despite the lurking menace in his words. 'Come on, old pal,' he encouraged. 'Show me where it is. First drop that rifle, will you? It makes me nervous.'

The rifle dropped from my hands. It was no time to argue with the madman with the Colt.

'Fine,' Andy said. And damn him, he laughed! It was all a game with Andy. Even when it came to life and death it was still a game. I had long ago decided that he did not care if he lived or died — or that he did not believe that he could ever die. Nothing makes a man more dangerous.

'Why did you start down this road, Andy?' I asked. Taking a chance I turned toward him. He was smiling. Good old Andy. There was a streak of blood high on his shoulder where I had tagged him with my rifle shot.

'What do you mean? Oh,' he said, as if finally taking my meaning. He looked thoughtful as he said, 'Why? Look at what we were, Keogh. Where we were going. We were nothing but two saddle tramps going nowhere, getting nothing for our labor half the time. It all came to me back at the old Pocono Ranch. Slattery trying to short us on our wages — how many times has that happened to us? And we would just swallow it, fork our broncs and drag the line one more time.

'You know what, Keogh? When I scalped old Barry Slattery for his stash of money, it felt good! To hell with him, anyway.'

'But later, Andy . . . killing that farmer. Taking the women. That is what tore us apart.'

'Keogh, old friend!' Andy said, with his hat tipped back, his dark curly hair tumbling out. 'You know I didn't mean to shoot that sodbuster. You were there!'

'He died,' I pointed out.

'He died and that made us wanted men, Keogh.' Andy was briefly angry. 'Over trouble we didn't start. I was only playing with Eva — you know me. Later, well, him — ' he gestured toward the dead body of Bull Mosely, 'he caught up with me, and it seemed like time to make a deal or get my neck stretched. So we made a deal. You know all about that. Dumb clodhopper thought he was in love. Do you think Eva would ever have given into him? Good-looking woman that she is? I strung the man along, and he fell in with me on a promise.' Andy laughed again. 'Just a dumb old sodbuster. Believing a woman was worth all that. Keogh, there's no woman worth that, is there?' He paused. 'I forgot — that's where we differ, isn't it, Keogh? That girl, that Mary Lou, that's what brought us to this, isn't it?'

'It is.'

'It wasn't the gold, it wasn't *that* turned you against me — you just wanted the girl.'

'That's right.'

Andy shook his head indulgently as if to say that I was no smarter than Bull Mosely had been in his pursuit of Eva Pierce. Then he shrugged, 'Well, I guess you've got her now,' he said. Then he returned to the main subject.

'Keogh, dig out that gold and we'll split it down the middle. The way we've always done things, me and you. You'll make that Mary Lou a happy girl when you show up with half of that gold. What the hell,' Andy said with a bright, boyish smile, 'I'm still making a better cut than I would have done splitting it with those three plowboys.'

I wasn't sure how to play this. The simplest thing would have been to agree with Andy and show him where I had tucked the gold away. But what then? I could not believe there was any sincerity behind his vow to split the stolen money with me. He might just take a whim and merrily gun me down.

I knew Andy too well.

For whatever reason, Andy had left me with my waist gun. He knew that I was only an average shot when shooting right-handed, had seen that I couldn't hit the side of a barn with my left. Maybe it hadn't seemed worth the bother to him, with me under the gun and him in complete control.

My second option, therefore, was to try to draw my Colt and fire before Andy could pump me full of lead. That really was no option at all, and he knew it.

'All right, Andy. Let's split it up. I'll show you where I hid it.'

'Now you're talking sense, Keogh. We've ridden too many trails together to have it end dirty. Let's dig it out and we can both get on our own ways — you with the filly, me for Mexico.'

We walked through the brush into the open clearing. The flies, I noticed, had begun to gather around Mosely's body, walking over his eyes. Was that to be my fate the minute I turned the gold up?

I hesitated as we entered the campsite, looking around as if I had lost my bearings. 'It was full dark, Andy,' I said, playing for time. Waiting for what? No one was coming to help me, it was just me and the killer alone on the plains. There was a strange glaze in Andy's eyes now, and I knew. No matter what I did he was going to kill me.

It is a strange feeling that comes over a man when he knows that death is inevitable. Not panic, fear or hysterical pleas to the Lord. Death is there, that is all and there is only the quiet submission to the fact that our life spans are limited. It didn't matter anymore: let him have the gold. Andy's own life was certain to be short the wild way he lived. Let him have his moment before the flies covered *his* eyes. I was too world-weary to care about trivial things like shiny metal any longer.

'The rock over there, Andy. There's a crease in it. I stuffed the saddlebags in there.'

'Truth, Keogh?' he asked. He could not kill me until he was sure of finding the gold.

'Have your look,' I said wearily, and he eased toward the mossy boulder, his Colt trained on me all the way. His hand searched the crevice, found

193

leather strapping. His face became triumphant, somehow boyish again. His favorite lost toy had been recovered.

'Let me go now, Andy,' I tried.

'Keogh!' Andy stood, holding the heavy pouches. 'Every time I turn around, there you are. You just keep dogging my trail. In Mexico I'd have to keep an eye out for you. You're always there! I'm sorry,' he said, not looking a bit sorry as his gun muzzle rose again in my direction.

The hoofbeats of the approaching horse were sharp and clear and Andy spun to face the rider. I recognized the chestnut instantly and fear rose and lodged in my throat. It was Marly, and Andy Givens's was going to shoot her down!

I spun, pawed clumsily at my left-hand gun, brought it up just as Andy Givens squeezed the trigger. My fumbling draw was as slow as a dream response, my thumb across the hammer was slow to ratchet the single-action, but as Andy's second shot roared out, I trued my aim and the bullet from my Colt hammered a .44 slug into his throat. Andy threw his gun aside, clutched at his terribly bleeding throat with both hands and staggered away across the camp.

He fell, dead, not five feet from where Bull Mosely lay.

I was angry. I was furious. Blood seemed to fill my eyes. I stormed toward the chestnut where Marly, wide-eyed, pale and shaken, still sat her saddle.

'Get down from there!' I shouted, my voice trembling and crazily pitched. And I half-dragged her from the horse. I had her in front of me, her shoulders tightly gripped. I shook her so that her head bobbed back and forth.

'Are you plain crazy, Marly! What are you doing out here. Are you crazy!'

'Yes, I guess so,' she said in a small voice. 'And what about you, Corey? Aren't you a little crazy, too? The things you've done.'

As my fear for her settled slowly, so

slowly, my limbs seemed to go weak all at once. It was Marly who supported me as we stumbled, staggered back to the very split boulder where the gold had been concealed. We sat side by side, saying nothing. Marly rested her head on my shoulder and she lightly held my broken right hand. We did not speak. There was nothing left to be said. We did not hear the intruder approach us. I was not aware of his presence until his bass voice said quietly:

'A little falling out among thieves, is that it?'

I turned my head to see a tall, well set-up man with coppery hair and a silver badge pinned to his blue shirt.

'You could call it that,' I managed to say.

'You boys have given me a long run. The name's Frank Copperfield, US marshal out of Denver.'

11

They have a well-built jail in Denver. All red brick and iron and no one has ever cracked out of this heavily guarded institution, they tell me. Although the food was nothing but compone and bacon, they gave you enough of it to keep you alive. Until your trial, until, if you were charged with murder as I was, they came and took you away to the scaffold hidden in the square behind the buildings.

Murder was the charge. Killing a man named Miles Sturdevant in Tulip. Tulip wanted me back, but Denver had said that they would do the honors. In Tulip they had half a hundred witnesses to the incident. Two men had broken into a Grange dance, shot dead one of the local citizens through the door during their escape. One of them, most definitely, was the prisoner Corey

Keogh. It was a solid hanging charge.

I tried, honestly, to convince the magistrate that it was Andy Givens who had done the shooting, but he told me that blaming a dead man was the oldest dodge in the books. No one could be found as a witness as to who had actually pulled the trigger. Besides I was, if not the actual gunman, guilty by complicity.

The days plodded by and my mood stayed dark, I was plain hangdog and cared nothing for the world outside, except for Marly who never had come to visit me. The only benefit of being locked down and fed, given a cot of my own, was that my battered body had begun to heal. Little good it would do me to march healthy up the steps to meet the hangman on the scaffold.

About four days on I heard the jailer call my name and I rose to my feet to see Eva Pierce escorted by the US Marshal, Frank Copperfield, walking down the flagged corridor toward my cell. Eva had a subdued excitement in her eyes that I could not immediately understand. She half-whispered to me:

'Corey, Marly is waiting with all of her love.'

'She hasn't been here,' I growled.

'It's not allowed — unescorted women visiting a prisoner unless they're married to them.' Copperfield explained briefly.

'I just wanted to thank you,' Eva said. 'I've tried to talk to everybody, explain all that you did.'

'It wasn't much help, I take it.'

'We don't know yet, Corey. Not yet. Warren Travers has spoken up for you too.'

'Who?'

'The mine owner, you remember. He's told the judge how you recovered his gold shipment for him. He's even tendered a reward to you.'

'I haven't got any use for gold where they're sending me,' I said. It wasn't that I was mad at Eva, angry with the world, I was just too tired to care about matters beyond my cell walls. They seemed to have little relevance to my small reality.

Copperfield took Eva aside for a moment and spoke quietly to her. She nodded, glanced at me and turned to leave. Copperfield's hand lingered on her shoulder reassuringly. The tall, substantial marshal approached my cell again.

'Keogh,' he said when we were alone, 'Eva has told me everything you did for her. I love that woman and intend to marry her. If not for you ... ' He paused. 'I have a question to ask you — have you ever been in Denver before?'

'No, sir. And I'm sorry I ever saw this city.'

'Are you sure you've never been here, Mr Keogh?'

I looked at him dumbly through the iron bars, not knowing what he was driving at.

'Why do you ask me?' I inquired cautiously. Were they trying to stick me with some other crime that had been committed here?

'Maybe you have been — once,' Copperfield said, looking around. He went on more quietly. 'Are you sure that you don't remember the day I deputized you and sent you out after Andy Givens and his gang? In my office alone with me. We swore to keep it secret so that word couldn't somehow leak out that you were a deputy marshal.'

I stared at the intent face of the lawman. I frowned; smiled. 'Oh, that,' I replied. 'Well, Copperfield, you said that we were to keep that strictly between ourselves. I didn't want to break the bond of silence until you authorized it.'

Copperfield nodded. The corner of his mouth twitched into a partial smile. He briefly touched the hand I was gripping the cold steel bars with, turned and walked away, striding purposefully down the long corridor, boot heels ringing on the stone flagging.

It was another two days until I

stepped out into the brilliant Colorado sunshine, blinked and took a full, free breath of mountain air. Marly was there, waiting.

Her eyes were brighter than the sky, and the scent of her was more invigorating than the spring breeze rolling down from the Rocky Mountain uplands. She clung to me and cried a little. I stroked her hair, unable to speak for a long while.

When passing people began to pause and stare, she drew away, holding both of my hands.

'What now?' I asked.

'What now?' she repeated. 'Well, Warren Travers has offered you a reward for recovery of the gold. You won't have to do anything for a while.'

'I can't just sit and do nothing,' I said, still clinging to her hand. 'A man needs to work.' I turned over my broken right hand. 'I'm done as a cowboy.'

'I guess you are,' Marly said. 'There's other jobs, Corey. For instance, the stage line has an opening for a line detective — and you have half a dozen good references for the position.'

'Do I?' I frowned. 'I don't know if I'd like that work, Marly. I'd have to think on it.'

'No one said you have to decide today, right now.' She smiled again and took my elbow, steering me along the bustling street. I slowed her long enough to ask:

'Where are you taking me, Marly?'

'We can't be late!' she answered. 'This is Copperfield and Eva's wedding day!'

She started away again, but I stopped her and looking down into her shining eyes, asked, 'This preacher who's marrying them, Marly, do you think he would charge much more for a double wedding?'

KILLER'S CREEK

David Bingley

It was named Killer's Creek when a child was killed in a fire. Henry Walton took the blame, instead of Doctor Rudge's wayward son, Jerry. Henry, when he was forced to leave Stillwater, formed a travelling circus. But Jerry Rudge reappeared in Chaparral, Utah, bringing trouble . . . The fire destroyed the rolling stock and Henry had to sell out. He rode the vengeance trail to Stillwater. Nothing could stop this lethal clash, or prevent Killer's Creek claiming a second victim.

LAST MAN RIDING

Clayton Nash

Too many dead men, too many posses, too many bullet wounds — so Brett McCabe decided to quit Tad Ripley's wild bunch. It should have been easy: Ripley was headed for certain death at the hands of Hank Bolan's posse. But, one good deed by McCabe nearly made it impossible. And, as always, the only way to settle things was in gunsmoke . . .

RIDERS FROM HELL

Lee Lejeune

It is the 1880s. Tom and Marie Flint have moved to New Mexico and run a thriving cattle business. Then, in El Jango, two fleeing bank robbers murder Flint's elder son when they hold up the Santa Fe stage. The killers, intent on revenge for past events, call themselves The Regulators. They want to destroy the Flint family. Up against the so-called Regulators, Tom and his younger son Jason fight a desperate battle to the death. But whose death?

THE KILLER'S BRAND

Terrell L. Bowers

Dace Kelly is released from prison on the condition that he helps the warden's sister save her ranch outside Tolerance, Colorado. He and the Professor, who is also being released, ride there together. But Dace faces problems aplenty: the warden's sister doesn't want Dace there, a gunman is after him and a powerful rancher is after the lady's ranch. Then there's someone intent on seeing the Professor dead ... Maybe Dace would have been a whole lot safer staying in prison!

KILL OR BE KILLED

Corba Sunman

Chet Walker returns to Kansas when his brother Burt faces trouble at the Flying W. Chet, after five years in Montana, accepts that Burt won the girl they both love, but he's unprepared for the trouble awaiting him. He becomes the target of gunfire as soon as he arrives. It seems that every man's hand is against him as he fights back. He must survive the mayhem and confront the crooks behind the plot to take over the range.

LAST CHANCE SALOON

Ross Morton

The Bethesda Falls stage is robbed and Ruth Monroe, the stage depot owner, is being coerced into selling up by local tycoon, Zachary Smith. Meanwhile Daniel McAlister arrives to wed Virginia, the saloon's wheel-of-fortune operator. Daniel hits a winning streak but is bushwhacked and robbed. Virginia is determined to stand by Daniel — ducking flying bullets if necessary as she and Daniel side with Ruth against Smith and his gunslingers. A deadly show-down will end it, one way or another . . .